THE SHADOW RIDERS

Other books by Owen G. Irons:

Guns Along the Brazos
The Outrider

THE SHADOW RIDERS

•

Owen G. Irons

AVALON BOOKS
NEW YORK

Published by Thomas Bouregy & Co., Inc.
160 Madison Avenue, New York, NY 10016

Library of Congress Cataloging-In-Publication Data

Irons, Owen G.
   The shadow riders / Owen G. Irons.
      p. cm.
   ISBN 978-0-8034-9961-4 (hardcover : acid-free paper)
   I. Title.

   PS3559.R6S5   2009
   813'.54—dc22

                                    2009004632

PRINTED IN THE UNITED STATES OF AMERICA
ON ACID-FREE PAPER
BY HADDON CRAFTSMEN, BLOOMSBURG, PENNSYLVANIA

Chapter One

Tyrone Cannfield didn't want to attack Sergeant Trammel. In fact he sort of liked the gloomy red-headed sergeant. But there always came a time when obligation outweighed friendship. From his cot in the barracks, Cannfield watched the slow approach of the heavy drill sergeant. Trammel had a knobby chin, a bulbous nose and sad, pouched eyes set too close together. There was a spark of anger in Trammel's glance. The NCO disliked trouble, problems with his troopers, but he was willing to take a deep breath, sigh and take care of business when the time came. His wide shadow spread itself over Cannfield as he approached the bunk.

"Didn't you hear the bugle blowing assembly?" Trammel asked with gentle menace.

"I heard it. I'm comfortable here," Cannfield said, yawning. His hands were clasped behind his head. His eyes only flickered toward Trammel and then resumed gazing at the ceiling.

The gentleness went out of Trammel's voice.

"Get up, get dressed and fall out, Cannfield!"

"If I don't?"

"You won't like the result," the drill sergeant promised. "Why do you have to make my days difficult, Cannfield?" Trammel asked, his tone nearly pleading. "I've done nothing to you."

"It's not you, Trammel. It's the army I don't like," Cannfield said, sitting up on his cot. He wore only his suspenders, blue trousers and a short-sleeved undershirt.

"See these?" Trammel asked tapping the five chevrons on his sleeve. "I *am* the army, and I'm telling you to fall out on the parade ground before this gets ugly."

The two men were alone in the barracks, but Cannfield heard a door open, and glancing that way, saw Wynn Corby, a nervous young recent recruit, watching the scene, his mouth open. Cannfield smiled and muttered, "It can't get much uglier than it is," closed his eyes and started to lie back on his cot again. Before his back touched the thin mattress, Sergeant Trammel's big hands caught Ty by the arms and with one violent, wrenching motion, Cannfield was thrown to the plank floor beside his bunk.

He sat up slowly, wiping the back of his hand across his mouth. He grinned and said, "Now this is going to get interesting."

Trammel, all of the good humor in his eyes darkened to bitter resolve, waited for Cannfield to rise. The sergeant's big fists were clenched as he hovered over the soldier.

"You going to do it now?" Trammel asked, his voice suddenly hoarse.

"Sure I am—now," Ty said, and before Trammel could react, the soldier gathered himself and launched his body into Trammel's, driving the big NCO across the aisle to slam into another trooper's neatly made bunk. Together they rolled from it onto the floor, both men winging punches as they went down.

There was a shout from across the barracks pleading with them to stop fighting, but Cannfield had no intention of stopping now. The job had to be done good and proper if he was to achieve what he had in mind.

Trammel was big and he was strong. Two pile-driving blows to Cannfield's ribs drove the wind from him, but did little to slow down Ty's wild assault on the NCO. He jabbed his left twice into Trammel's wide face, snapping the sergeant's head back. Trammel grunted with surprise, then came forward with grim determination. Ty backed away and found himself against the barracks wall.

"Stop it!" someone called again from the door to the building. The voice belonged to Wynn Corby and as Ty glanced that way he saw the young trooper rush toward the combatants, his bootheels thudding against the planking.

Ty regretted having looked away, for Sergeant Trammel took advantage of the momentary distraction to slam his bulky forearm into Ty's face. Ty's head rocked back against the wall of the barracks and hot blood began streaming from both nostrils. Ty ducked, bobbed his head and came up throwing a right hook that landed square on Trammel's ear.

Amazingly, Corby had launched himself into the fray. The young trooper was on Trammel's back, his thin arms wrapped around the NCO's chest. Trammel threw an elbow back into Corby's side and then took one of the soldier's arms and flung him aside as easily as if he were a child.

Before Corby could rise from his sprawled position Ty put a halt to matters. He hadn't intended to get Corby involved in this fight. The kid could get himself seriously hurt if he tried to interfere with the two brawling soldiers again. Ty put his hands up slowly, his eyes fixed on Trammel's.

"I guess I've had enough, Sarge," Ty said, using his wrist to wipe some of the blood from his nose and mouth. For a moment Ty thought that Trammel was going to hit him again for good luck, but slowly the NCO's fists lowered and some measure of calm returned to his angry features.

"I wish to hell you'd'a stopped earlier, Cannfield," Trammel said with a shadow of regret. "You've left me no choice about matters."

Trammel stepped back, unsnapped the flap on his holster and drew his service revolver. "You're going to see Colonel Toomey. You and your pal here." With that, Trammel leaned down, gripped Corby's collar and yanked him to his feet. The freckled kid stood there shaking, his face as pale as death.

"He has nothing to do with this," Ty said. "You heard him—he was only trying to stop it."

Trammel's eyes were calm, but fixed. "He should have found another way to try it besides jumping me."

"I tell you he wasn't . . ."

"Cannfield, save it for the colonel," Trammel replied.

He gestured with the muzzle of his pistol for Ty to step into the center aisle of the barracks. Then, marching Ty at gunpoint, half-dragging the staggering Corby along by the collar of his tunic, they made their way out of the building into the harsh light of the Arizona morning.

On the parade ground the rest of the platoon stood in a loose formation, awaiting the return of Sergeant Trammel. Their attention was immediately captured by the sight of their drill sergeant, pistol drawn, nudging Cannfield toward the headquarters building, his left hand gripping the pathetically struggling Corby's collar. All eyes were on the three passing men. There was a flurry of murmured words, a catcall or two, and several men laughed out loud until the corporal of the guard shouted them to silence.

Cannfield's boots kicked up puffs of fine white dust as he was marched toward the low adobe headquarters building. There wasn't much to Camp Grant. A palisade constructed of sharpened lodgepole-pines surrounded the cluster of adobe buildings—barracks, headquarters building, a smith's shack, sutler's store and the officer's private quarters. In time the desert would reclaim the site. The rain, infrequent as it was, would wash the adobe bricks away, returning them to the mud they had been formed from. The army would not remain here long, and when they were gone the palisade would be scavenged for firewood by the few local ranchers or by the blanket Indians—members of the Yuma tribe—who made their camp near the army post for protection against the savage Apaches living in the desert and sheltering hills beyond.

Cannfield had time to look up at those hills, folded and

tormented by the eons. They crowded near Camp Grant. They were gray now, covered only by dry purple sage and other dormant chaparral. Along the high ridges, here and there, were twisted, wind-tormented pinyon pines. The scent of the Gila River, beyond the walls of the fort, was heavy and brackish.

The hot desert wind, which had been quiet, now began to gust fitfully through the camp, pressing Cannfield's shirt against his back, drying the perspiration that had been clinging there.

"Step up, Cannfield," Trammel said as they reached the porch of the headquarters building. The trio passed through the narrow band of shade cast by the wooden awning and into the relative coolness of the adobe building.

The first sergeant, McCrory, looked up unhappily from his desk work and demanded, "What's this, Trammel?"

"Two men who assaulted me in the barracks, Mac." He nodded at each of them in turn. "Corby . . . and you know Private Tyrone Cannfield, of course."

"You're back again, are you Cannfield?" the thick-chested first sergeant said, rising behind his desk. "It seems to me that you were warned the last time that we would not be putting up with any more of your antics."

Cannfield was silent. Sergeant McCrory sighed heavily, rolled down the cuffs of his shirt and buttoned them before walking to the colonel's office door.

"This isn't going to go easy this time," Trammel said in a low voice. Again, Cannfield made no reply.

"What'll they do to us?" Corby asked in a shaky voice.

Not unkindly, Trammel answered, "It'll be the hotbox

and then hard labor this time." A strangled groan escaped from Corby's throat. He looked around desperately.

"I told you the kid wasn't involved," Ty told Trammel again. "He was only trying to stop the fight. If you would tell the colonel that . . ."

"I can only tell the colonel what happened," Trammel said stiffly, "not what Corby was thinking when he jumped a non-commissioned officer."

"You know . . ." Cannfield began, trying to plead Corby's case again, but it was too late. The door to Colonel Toomey's office was open and Sergeant McCrory stood with his back against it. He gestured with a slight nod of his head and Trammel escorted the two troopers toward the commanding officer's office.

It was going to be bad, very bad, Ty knew immediately as they stepped into the colonel's office. Sitting in a corner chair was Lieutenant Deveraux. His long face ended at a sharp chin which was cleft as deeply as if a saber had done it. His eyes were small, dark, and expressionless. The ends of his black mustache dropped an inch or so below his small, tightly compressed mouth. Deveraux never let his gaze wander from Ty's face.

It was going to be bad.

Behind the desk sat Colonel Richard Toomey, a colorless man whose body seemed almost shapeless beneath his tunic. Obviously too old for his position, he was hanging on until he could pension out. Ty had never seen the cavalry officer on a horse. In fact Toomey was seldom seen outside at all except when moving from his office to his quarters where his equally shapeless wife, a grim woman with tightly braided and coiled yellow-gray hair, shared his colorless life.

"Private Tyrone Cannfield and Private Wynn Corby," First Sergeant McCrory announced. He then let Trammel explain the charges against the troopers. To give the man his due, Ty thought that Trammel was quite reasonable and fair in his telling of the events in the barracks, considering that Ty had assaulted the NCO with premeditation and absolutely no provocation. Corby's case was a completely different matter. When Trammel had finished, Ty tried to explain Corby's involvement in the fight.

"Sir, Private Corby was only trying . . ."

"Be quiet, Cannfield," Lieutenant Deveraux ordered, rising to his feet to study Ty more closely. "No one invited you to speak."

Corby glanced at Ty, his pale eyes frightened and imploring. His knees continued to wobble so much he had trouble remaining at attention.

Colonel Toomey rubbed his eyes with his fingers. It was the weary gesture of a man who does not care for any interruption of what should have been, by this time of life, a well-ordered, peaceful existence. He had only three months left to serve before he could retire. Why did they have to send him malcontents and troublemakers like Cannfield?

Colonel Toomey barely glanced at the two accused men throughout the interview. Lieutenant Deveraux, on the other hand, continued to glare at Cannfield, his malice unconcealed. The two men were nearly exact opposites, Ty thought. The colonel slow, burdened by undefined sorrow, slow to make decisions and slow to act. Deveraux, on the other hand, was narrowly built, tense as a tiger and eager to act. It was well-known that Deveraux was waiting—impatiently—for the colonel to retire so that he could pin on his captain's bars and assume command of Camp Grant.

Deveraux was harsh and unyielding. It was said that his nightly prayer was for the Apaches to start up trouble so that he could gain glory in the field.

The colonel turned his watery eyes on Deveraux and asked, "Lieutenant?" as if the decision should be the younger officer's and not his.

"I'll take care of it, sir," Deveraux said with the grace of a rattlesnake. "That will be all, Sergeant Trammel," he said, dismissing the drill sergeant. "Find Corporal Boggs and Sullivan and send them over to me."

"Yes, sir," Trammel said without pleasure. Boggs was in charge of the stockade. Sullivan was his right-hand man. Both were known to be vicious when the mood struck them. Trammel saluted and went out, leaving the door open.

"Gentlemen," Deveraux said to Ty and Corby, "let's go."

Colonel Toomey looked both worried and relieved as salutes were exchanged and Lieutenant Deveraux ushered the prisoners out of the office and into the orderly room. Sergeant McCrory glanced up once from his daily reports, then resumed working.

Corby was more than shaken. He seemed ready to collapse. With a wild look in his eyes he stepped toward Lieutenant Deveraux, extending a pleading arm. "Sir, if you would only let me explain what . . ."

Deveraux kicked him sharply on the kneecap and the young trooper went down hard. He lay on the wooden floor, clutching his knee, his mouth working like a dying fish. Ty had to fight the urge to fly at Deveraux. It would have been pointless. The officer had his hand on his service revolver and First Sergeant McCrory, alerted by the scuffle, looked ready to join in any fight.

Deveraux, damn him, was smiling as Wynn struggled to rise.

The outer door opened behind Ty and he glanced that way to see Corporal Boggs and Private First Class Dana Sullivan enter. Boggs carried a shotgun in the crook of his arm; Sullivan had leg irons thrown over his shoulder. Lieutenant Deveraux looked at Ty and Corby through eyelids drawn to mere slits.

"Two for the hotbox," Deveraux said and Boggs nodded with seeming pleasure. The two prisoners were taken away in manacles. This time when they crossed the parade ground there was no laughter from the watching troopers, but only the silence of pity.

Day lingered interminably. The sun rose higher and the heat in the six-by-six-by-four foot hotbox where Cannfield and Corby were confined continued to rise. Corby lay in a tangle, his throbbing knee bringing moans of pain to his lips. The young trooper was injured, defeated and held no hope for the future. At the least after his sentence was done he would be drummed out of the army—if he made it that long. Ahead of them once they were released from the hotbox lay months of hard labor beneath the torrid Arizona sun. Corby would be lucky to survive.

The kid had been the butt of barracks jokes for a long time. Small, uncertain, he did not endure the constant ribbing of the other troopers well. He had attached himself to Cannfield after Ty had extricated him from a hazing at the hands of the other soldiers. That was why, Ty supposed, Corby had unwisely thrown himself into the fight with Sergeant Trammel. Now the young man's loyalty to Ty would likely mean the end of his career if not the finish of his short life.

Corby had joined the army as soon as he reached enlistment age, sure that the West was the place for him, certain that he would become a man among men. Instead he had become a foil for the rough jokes of the hardened Indian fighters in the platoon.

Ty tried to roll over to shift his position. In the close confines of the double casket, it was not easy, shackled as he was. Sweat permeated his clothing, stung his eyes, trickled annoyingly down into one ear.

Ty's own official record read far different from Corby's. He was a conscript, not an enlistee. His military file reflected that of a man with a criminal background, given the choice by a civilian judge of entering the army or serving time in the Arizona State Prison at Yuma, a common practice at that time. The army needed more soldiers than they could entice; the local authorities were happy just to move their troublemakers out of their jurisdiction.

Ty's record showed him to be just that—a troublemaker. In fact he had arrived at Camp Grant after being transferred from Fort Bowie following an incident involving an assault on an officer. The commanding officer at Fort Bowie had also found it simpler to transfer Ty than to deal with him.

The never-ending day, finally exhausted, began to slip

toward dusk. There was a narrow band of violet showing through the six-inch-high slit of a window in the hotbox, cut through the wooden walls only to keep the prisoners from suffocating. Day was ending; the temperature was not falling, however. Not yet. It would remain high, stifling until just before dawn. Then when some relief began to cool them enough to allow sleep, sunrise would arrive on the heels of night, and the cycle would continue.

Corby continued to groan. Now and then a sob would escape from his throat. The young trooper was in utter misery. His past was insubstantial, his future bleak and unpromising. The present was only a wreath of pain and discomfort laid over his miserable tomb.

Ty had deep sympathy for the younger soldier. As for himself, he was quite pleased with the way matters were proceeding. The task he had been assigned was progressing exactly as planned.

Chapter Two

Not ten days earlier as Phoenix lay blistering beneath the glare of the white midday sun, Tyrone had made his way across a dusty downtown street and into the wide, low-ceilinged offices of Ethan Payne. There was no one waiting to meet him, and the door to the inner office was closed. Ty settled in to wait, crossing his legs and placing his hat on one knee. Ten minutes later two rough-looking, trail-dusty men Ty didn't know exited the inner room and passed by, giving him vaguely suspicious glances.

The man standing in the doorway behind them grinned, causing his gray handlebar mustache to twitch a little. Tall, lean, his thinning dark hair slicked back, Ethan looked much the same as Ty remembered him.

"Tyrone! Glad you decided to come up here. Come on in; let's have a talk."

Ty rose, crossed the floor of the outer office, shook

Payne's powerful hand firmly and followed him into the room. The mustached man sat behind his desk and Ty took a wooden chair opposite. Looking around, Ty saw crossed sabers and a map of Arizona territory on one wall, a territorial flag and a portrait of President Grant on another. Outside the window a mockingbird had perched on the sill to look in, its gray head cocked, eye bright and curious. On the desk was an engraved brass plaque which read *Capt. E. Payne—Arizona Rangers.*

"What is it then, Ethan?" Ty asked without prelude. "You said you needed me. What for?"

Payne smiled with one side of his mouth. A cigar had been planted in the other half. He lit the cigar slowly and leaned back in his chair, studying Cannfield's face.

"How would you feel about joining the army?" The Arizona Ranger asked. Ty laughed out loud.

"About the way you think I'd feel," he replied. "Is that a joke, Ethan?"

"Hardly," Captain Payne said seriously. He tapped the ash from his cigar into a pewter ashtray. Beyond the window, the mockingbird gave a scolding cry and flew away on banded wings. Payne continued to study Ty's face, his eyes, wondering if he was looking at the same man who had served so valiantly under him and McCulloch in the Texas Rangers, or if something had been taken out of Cannfield after the murder of his young wife—killed by unknown assailants while Payne and Ty, along with twenty-four other rangers were off scouting the border following several incidents involving a band of renegade Comanches.

Ty had been a bold, nearly reckless Texas Ranger in those days, a constant smile on his lips, steady in action, good with his guns, well-liked by all of the men. After the murder of Kathleen, Ty had changed, not a little, not gradually, but overnight and to the extreme. He had retained his recklessness, but there was a grim combativeness about him. He had remained a week longer in the Rangers after Kathleen's death, then abruptly resigned. "To go hunting," Ty had written as the reason for leaving the unit on his resignation papers. Every man in the Rangers knew exactly who Ty meant to hunt, track down and kill.

Where Ty had been the following year no one knew; it was known that he had never found his man. But it had been reported to Captain Payne that Ty had managed to fight his way out of the self-destructive hatred he had been carrying. Although he had changed unalterably and still smiled less frequently, he had found a way to make his anger more manageable as time passed.

The Ty Cannfield who now sat across the desk from Payne was not the same youngster he had ridden with in the Rangers, but neither was he a wild-eyed hunter bent solely on revenge. Was he ready to go to work again? This time for the newly-formed Arizona Rangers that had been formed in the territory based on the Texas model? Payne asked him directly.

"We can use your help, Ty . . . if you're willing to work for me."

"What was it you were saying about joining the army?" Ty asked, leaning forward slightly in his chair. He had not answered Captain Payne's question directly. He hadn't needed to. His refusal would have taken the form of smiling, shaking his head and walking away from the building.

"That is what I am asking you to do," Payne said, relighting his cigar which had gone cold. "Not as an actual enlistee, of course. There are ways of fabricating a military record for you. The army is offering its full cooperation—the problem is of as much concern to them as it is to us."

"The problem being . . . ?" Ty leaned back again in his chair, seeming to relax. His eyes held fierce concentration.

Captain Payne explained. "There is a band of outlaws, a large band, conducting raids in the territory. Their activities are centered around Tucson, although they have struck far and wide when the opportunity presented itself. Banks are their target of preference. Stagecoaches are hit constantly. They're not above emptying out gun shops or general stores in the middle of the night to resupply themselves."

"Are you talking about Comancheros?" Ty asked, referring to bands of men composed of ex-Confederates, renegade Indians, Mexicans and escaped slaves who had come together in recent years to ravage isolated communities.

"No," Payne said, "the army has mostly run the Comancheros out of business, or sent them scurrying for the border. These men—we are calling them Shadow Riders—are of a different ilk. The army has had little luck fighting them for reasons I will go into later. The Shadow Riders seem to be made up of about ninety per cent army deserters. The disaffected, those who can't take life on a lonely desert outpost, malcontents. Most of them are conscripts, sent to the army by well-meaning Eastern judges in hopes that the military can straighten them out where civilian society could not."

"How many are there?" Ty asked.

"No one really knows. The number of soldiers who desert the army in the Western lands is huge. Out on patrol, who's to stop a man from simply riding to the horizon and starting a new life? What's the hope that the army, even had they the inclination, could track down a single soldier lost in the vastness of the territory?"

"But these men, these Shadow Riders, are different. Far from disappearing into the desert, they ride together, advertise themselves by committing crimes." Ty was baffled. "Why isn't this a military matter, Ethan?"

Ethan smiled without humor. His cigar had gone cold again, but he did not relight it this time. "Because it may be that some active enlisted men, even officers, are engaged in the recruiting of the outlaws, Ty. Involved in planning their raids. The Shadow Riders always seem to know where the army will *not* be conducting operations."

"But why would they . . . ?"

"There's money involved, Ty. A lot of money, and cash has always been effective at eroding men's consciences."

"I see," Ty said thoughtfully. Perhaps he was ignorant, idealistic, but the idea of a man turning traitor on his own unit was unthinkable. Payne went on.

"The top generals are pulling out their hair; they have vowed to clean this up one way or the other. With few options, they came to the Rangers, and together we have devised a plan which has a chance—a slim chance—of working."

"This is where I come in, I suppose," Ty said doubtfully. His eyes narrowed with thought and he shook his head slightly. "I am a malcontented soldier. I find some way to fall in with the Shadow Riders and point you to their hide-out." He paused. "Sounds chancy to me. I don't like it, Ethan."

"I don't like it much myself," Captain Payne said. "But someone has to be inside, someone who can locate their encampment for us—we know they have a permanent base from the sorts of materials they have occasionally stolen. Farming implements, lumber, woodworking tools, hard-ware."

"There might be some local rancher sheltering them, a landholder who lives in an isolated area."

"We think that is very possible," Payne agreed.

"Any idea who?" Ty asked.

"No. If we had an idea, we'd be following it up."

"You must be trying," Ty said.

"*Of course!* You saw those exhausted rangers who were leaving my office. Sperry and Nichols, two of my best men. They've been scouting the area around Tucson for three weeks. Not a trace of the outlaws although the gang hit two banks in the area during that time. What we've been trying is just not working. Now we want to try to infiltrate the Shadow Riders."

Ty was silent for a long while. The mockingbird had returned for a second visit. Beyond the perched bird a dust devil raced silently past, carrying a funnel of light dust toward the gray rocky hills. It was a dangerous plan the Rangers had in mind. It could be called suicidal. If a rat were discovered among them, the outlaws would no doubt kill him. Was that why Captain Payne had thought of Ty? Perhaps the way he had lived the past year made them think that he *was* suicidal. He had been—almost—after Kathleen had been killed. His life had seemed to have no meaning left at all then. Perhaps it had a little more now.

"What have I got to lose?" Ty said with a thin smile. "Tell me more."

Captain Payne took only half an hour to explain to Ty exactly what was needed—chiefly information about the home base of the Shadow Riders, and any information concerning when and where they would strike again so the Rangers could lay an ambush for the marauding band.

"You will have one ally in the gang," Payne told Ty. "If he has not already been caught. An informant who gave his name only as 'Bert' has managed to pass some information to us, unfortunately not enough to do the Shadow Riders any permanent damage. Bert does seem to have a line of communication that you can utilize if and when you come up with news concerning their plans.

"And he is . . . ?" Ty asked.

"We know nothing at all about Bert, who he is, why he has sent messages to us. Whether you trust him or not will be for you to decide. This may be a lengthy operation, Ty. There will certainly be some sort of probation period in which you will have to prove yourself—possibly in ways that will be . . . distasteful, to say the least."

"I understand," Ty said, considering what sort of initiation the outlaws might demand. Lifting his eyes he asked, "How am I supposed to make contact with these men in the first place?"

Payne lit his cigar and grinned. "That is the simple part, Ty. They actively recruit soldiers who are troublemakers, criminal material. All you need to do is make yourself into the most disagreeable, disaffected trooper at Camp Grant. You won't have to find them; they'll find you."

Ty thought he'd done as much as possible to aggravate the army and to present himself as a prime candidate for the Shadow Riders. Now there was nothing to do but wait. It was on the morning of what would have been his and Wynn Corby's sixth day in the hotbox that the heavy plank door opened to the accompanying complaint of its heavy iron hinges. The blinding glare of white desert light flooded the cage.

"*Get up!*" the hoarse voice of PFC Sullivan ordered. He was only a black silhouette against the stunning brightness of the desert behind him. His foot nudged the sole of Ty's boot. "Up, trooper. You too, Corby!"

The young soldier sat up rubbing his eyes. He crawled on hands and knees to the low doorway and Ty followed. Ty made no sudden moves. His eyes had adjusted well enough to see the heavy, menacing club in Sullivan's hand.

Outside, Ty rose unsteadily. Five days in the hotbox, barely able to stretch his muscles, had left him feeling nerveless. He rubbed his legs, trying to improve his circulation. Looking down, he saw that Corby was unable to rise from the ground on his own, so he helped the young man to his feet where he wavered unsteadily like a reed in the wind.

There were two other soldiers holding Springfield rifles behind Sullivan, their eyes watchful and hard.

"Let's go," Sullivan said.

"Where?" Corby managed to ask in a strangled voice. His eyes were as apprehensive as if he expected a firing squad.

"Regular stockade," Sullivan answered impatiently. He spun on his heel and started marching along the inner wall of the stockade toward the punishment barracks which stood beyond the stables. Ty moved unsteadily, his legs still unused to motion. Corby had to hold onto Ty's arm for support. The two guards behind them kept poking them with their rifle barrels, prodding them on.

Corby's watery eyes looked up at Ty from under a fringe of unwashed hair and he whispered hopefully, "The worst is over now."

Ty was less than convinced, but he said nothing to the thin young soldier. The sun was brutally hot, reflecting off the white sand dunes beyond the post, carving deep shadowed clefts into the flanks of the chocolate-brown hills beyond. There were two more armed guards flanking the door to the punishment barracks. They stepped aside as Sullivan stepped up onto the porch, and approached the heavy door with an iron key.

"Two more guests," he said to the watching soldiers.

"We've been expecting them," one of the troopers replied in a tone that carried an underlying threat.

Inside the barracks it was relatively cool. There was little light, only that knifing through to the interior from a row of three slit windows high on the wall. Each bunk had a chain and ankle band tethered to it for restraining the prisoners at night. There were also two barred rooms at the end of the barracks where they were led.

Their shackles, thankfully, were finally removed as they were pushed into one of these small cells. Ten by ten at the most, they were able to stand up for the first time in nearly a week. Even more welcome were two iron cots placed along facing walls. By comparison to what they had suffered, it was an ascent to paradise.

The cell smelled of sweat, sickness and an unidentifiable musk. It was windowless, of course, but enough light bled through the barred observation portal in the door so that they could see each other's faces.

Corby looked like hell. Thin, haggard, beaten, his eyes sunken and despairing. Ty tried not to let his assessment show in his expression. "Sorry you got dragged into this, Wynn," he said honestly. "It was not my intention."

"It's all right, Ty," Corby said, raising a forgiving hand. "You're my friend. My only friend, I guess. At least you never rode me the way the others did." A hint of anger tinged his voice.

"Bastards, why do they do it?" Corby lowered his face into his hands.

"They don't mean it, Wynn," Ty said unconvincingly. "The new man is always hazed—anywhere you go, until they get tired of it or the next new man signs on."

"Why do they do it?" Wynn repeated as if he hadn't heard Ty. His hands fell away from his face and he lifted his eyes. "One day I'll get even with them. If I have to kill them." Corby's eyes had changed expression. Fear and anguish had been replaced by a smoldering anger. Ty feared that the young trooper was serious. He didn't want Wynn to dwell on that hastily uttered vow.

"Forget it. By now they will have," he advised Corby, but again his words seemed to fall on deaf ears.

Ty settled back on his bunk, hands clasped behind his head, staring at the unmoving bar-shadows on the wall. He intended to rest for as long as they would let him. He had no doubts as to what was to come. Corby also was considering their future.

"What are they going to do to us now, Ty?" he asked.

"You heard the sentence—hard labor. We'll be out in the sun from dawn to dusk. Probably making big rocks into little rocks with a sledge hammer. They've been working on a road to the river. It's difficult for the water wagons to make it through the sand, especially when they're loaded."

"I won't survive," Corby said miserably. "I can't! All day out there—swinging a sledge. I just can't make it, Ty."

"You'll make it," Ty answered. "You'll do fine. Anyway, it'll only be thirty days or so. Probably less for you."

"I'll never make it," Corby repeated miserably. Unfortunately, Ty agreed with the little man. It was called hard labor for a reason, and it took a strong man to survive that kind of work, especially under the relentless glare of the desert sun. Ty murmured a few more reassurances and then closed his eyes, not to sleep but to re-examine his mission. No one had contacted him yet. Would they now that he had been released from the hotbox? Or had Ethan, with the best of intentions, only succeeded in delivering him into a painful, hopeless situation?

Somehow Ty managed to fall asleep, a deep and mercifully dreamless sleep. It was not until sundown that he was awakened by the sound of work boots tramping into the barracks.

"What is it?" Corby asked.

"Work crew's back," Ty told him, shifting his position on the cot. Listening closely they could hear the dull complaints of the weary laborers, a word or two exchanged in low voices and later, as night settled and the barracks went dark, someone quietly sobbing.

It was still dark when the door to their cell swung open and Corporal Boggs entered with an armed trooper behind him. He held leg irons which he dropped on the floor. The heavy chains clanged like the bells of death, and he ordered the two to remain seated on their bunks while he fastened the manacles to their ankles.

"Get up, boys," Boggs said when he was through. "First day of work. Go along with this soldier; he'll issue you work boots and show you where you breakfast."

Boggs went out, leaving them to the silent soldier who had the black eyes and hawk nose of someone with Apache blood in his veins. He gestured with the muzzle of his rifle and Ty, followed by a trembling Corby, shuffled out of the room, their chains rattling on the floor.

"Pick 'em up," the soldier said, gesturing, and they reached down for their chains, hoisting them so they didn't clank against the wooden flooring.

Shod in work boots, they were taken to a twelve-byforty-foot room where the other prisoners were already hard at it, spooning thin gruel from their metal dishes like starving men. Few lifted their eyes to the new intakes; fewer showed any interest in them.

Outside they were assembled and counted as the first colors of dawn began to streak the peaks of the hills along the northern skyline. Before first light they were marched across the parade ground, passed through the double gates of the post and gathered around a wagon where each man was handed his tool for the day. A few of the older prisoners were given shovels. The usual implement was a twelve-pound sledgehammer. Most of these were not well-cared-for and many of the handles had weathered into dangerously splintered shafts.

By the time the sun had fully risen the temperature was already nearing triple digits on the thermometer. By the time they had begun swinging steel against solid granite boulders the yellow ball was like a branding iron against their backs. No one spoke. Rocks were broken. They were sorted and hauled away in barrows to be dumped on the roadbed. One man collapsed and was beaten to his feet. Ty worked on, steadily, wordlessly; he tried not to glance too often at Corby who was already wilting under the fiery sun, exhausted by the unceasing labor he was unaccustomed to.

At noon they stopped, leaning against a huge boulder which spread a ribbon of shadow against the heated earth. Each man was given one pint of water, a thick slice of yesterday's bread and allowed to rest for half an hour.

Ty watched Corby sitting loosely on the ground, hands wrapped around his knees, fingers clutching his uneaten bread. The kid had been right—he would never make it. And there was nothing Ty could do to help him, nothing at all.

In the evening, with the sun dropping behind the serrated hills, they deposited their tools in the wagon, marched wearily homeward, were counted again and served corn soup and bread before being locked onto their bunks in long, silent rows. Ty heard a man sobbing in the darkness. This time it was Corby.

On the third day as they ate their noontime meal, some voraciously, some apathetically, a trooper's shadow fell across Ty and he glanced up to see one of the soldiers assigned to guard the work crew. The trooper turned his head, looking toward the flowing silver river beyond. His lips barely moved as he said, "I can get you out of this, Cann-field. The army won't ever let up on you. I've seen your record. You're a habitual troublemaker."

"Yeah? How are you going to get me out of here?" Ty muttered with weary sarcasm although his heart rate had picked up in anticipation. Was this the moment he had been waiting for?

"Never mind that," the soldier said, still looking away. "Let's just say it can be done. I know where there's a better life. And they pay more than twenty-six dollars a month. A lot more."

"Is that so?" Ty said skeptically. He drank the last of the water in his steel canteen. "Show me."

"Be patient. Maybe tonight. Maybe tomorrow night. We can bust you out . . . unless you prefer it here," he said with a smirk.

"If you're on the level, I'll ride anywhere you like, friend. So long as it's away from the army."

"Far away," the soldier answered, turning his head to spit. "As far as you can get."

"One thing," Ty said, glancing at the sun-lashed, exhausted Corby. "Take the kid along, too."

"I don't know," the soldier said, biting at his lip. "He's in no shape to ride. Besides, we can only take a few men at a time. Any more than that and the army might figure it's worth mounting a patrol to come after us."

"Find a way," Ty said. "I'll see that the kid's ready."

"How?"

"From now on he's on extra rations. I'm going to give him most of my food and half of my water."

"You that fond of the kid?" the soldier asked with surprise.

"Just see that it's not more than a few days," Ty said.

"You can bank on it," the trooper promised. Then seeing another armed guard approaching, his voice changed and strengthened. "And the next time I tell you to do something, make sure you do it!" Then he tugged down his cap, turned and marched away down the hillslope.

Corby, disturbed by the guard's shouting, lifted red, weary eyes to Ty and asked, "What was all that about, Ty?"

"I wish I knew," Ty said thoughtfully, watching the retreating back of the guard. "Time's up," he added as the rest of the laborers struggled to their feet to begin the long afternoon of man-killing work. "Let's get to it before there's more trouble."

Ty considered the bargain he'd made with the nameless soldier as the torrid day slowly passed to the accompanying metronome of his sledgehammer ringing against granite. He had no desire to drag Corby along with him on an already-hazardous mission. But he knew full well what the young private's fate would be if he were left behind to try surviving on his own. He had, Ty believed, chosen the least deadly alternative.

There was no further contact from the Shadow Riders— if that was who had sent the message—over the next two days. Corby, protesting only mildly when Ty gave him his food, grew a little stronger as his ration increased by another half pint of water and an extra slice of bread at noontime, an additional bowl of corn soup for dinner. He was not filling out any, but his stringy body seemed more resilient now. Once in awhile he even found the strength to smile.

On the other hand, as a result of his generosity, Ty began to grow weaker. His stomach constantly growled and the sledgehammer grew heavier. He slept like a dead man when they returned to the punishment barracks at sundown.

The man rousing Ty from his sleep took a long time bringing him to alertness.

"It's tonight—get it?" a voice from out of the inky darkness of the night whispered into Ty's ear. "The barracks door will be open for five minutes only. You'll hear a coyote howl. That will be your signal to get up and get out. Don't hesitate or that door will lock again and stay locked."

The faceless man added, "Keep your little friend quiet and keep him moving."

Then Ty felt fingers working over the cuff of his trousers and he felt the manacle on his ankle release. It was lowered soundlessly to the floor. The shadowy figure moved on to Corby's bunk and Ty saw the faceless man working the key in his shackle. Corby was not roused by the contact and he slept on fitfully as his minacle was removed and placed aside.

Ty lay awake, staring at the ceiling. Beyond the walls of the barracks nothing stirred. There was no sound at all across the post. It was a dead, silent world smothered beneath the heavy weight of the black desert night. Ty clenched and unclenched his hands, moved his manacle-abraded ankle, testing it. And waited for the coyote to call.

Chapter Three

The call, when it came, sounded distant and muffled, but it was definitely a coyote howl—or rather a man imitating one. Ty wasted no time rolling from his bunk and slipping to Corby's side. Crouched against the floor, his eyes searching the shadows of the night, Ty shook Corby awake.

"What the . . . ?" Corby's sleep-stunned eyes managed to make out Ty's features in the dark. "What's going on?" he asked, too loudly.

Ty placed his hand over Corby's mouth. He whispered harshly, "Not another word. Grab your boots. We're leaving." Corby's mouth moved; he wanted to ask more questions, but instead he did as Ty commanded. Sitting up, Corby stuffed his feet into his work boots and stood, waiting.

Ty hesitated. It could be a trap. An excuse to shoot them

as escapees, but there would be no other time, no other chance to make a break for freedom. Ty eased through the row of sleeping men, Corby at his heels. Ty fingered the outer door lightly and felt it open at his prod. Glancing at a nervous Corby, he took a deep breath, opened the door wide and slipped into the night.

There was no guard on the porch. More than one soldier was making money off this operation, it seemed. Ty hesitated, not knowing which way to go. Suddenly a silhouette appeared to their left and a hand gestured the escaped men to follow. They slipped along the shadowed side of the barracks, moving past the empty horse corral. There was no need to caution them to silence. Ty could hear nothing but his own breathing and the faint sound of his leather boot soles whispering against the earth.

Their guide halted at the open double doors to the horse barn, a long, heavy-beamed building smelling of hay and manure. "Straight through," their guide hissed. "Out the small door in the back."

"We could just grab two horses," Corby said, clutching Ty's arm.

"And go where?" their usher said savagely. "They hear the horses moving, they come and kill you."

The moon had not yet risen, but now backlighted by the glow of a thousand stars, Ty could see their guide's profile plainly. It was the Apache-looking man who had issued them their work boots on their first day in the stockade. The man was already walking away from them; Ty and Corby followed along. The interior of the barn was deep in darkness. Rows of animal eyes peered at them as they made their way toward the small door beyond. The door was fixed with two huge brass padlocks. Both hasps hung open.

"Come on," the Indian whispered sharply.

Slipping through the door they paused for a moment and behind them Ty heard someone click the padlocks on the stable door shut again. Ahead now stood only the looming palisade and they crossed in a silent body to a Judas gate used by the kitchen help to pass out and dispose of mess hall garbage. This gate was also unlocked and they were through it in a minute, moving away from the fort, striding across desert sand. Ty and Corby continued to glance back, fearing pursuit, but there was none.

"Hurry up," the Indian said. They scurried up a sandy hill and down the other side which was studded with small, broken rocks. Below them, backlighted by the trace light of the sky, Ty could make out a long stand of willow trees crowding a bend in the Gila river. Unhesitatingly the Indian led the way through the willow brush and reeds until they came to a small clearing where a man in civilian clothes stood holding his horse's reins and the leads to three other ponies, none of them army stock.

"Took your time," the stranger muttered. He was wide and fairly short, Ty saw, wearing a wide-brimmed flop hat. Starlight reflected off a holstered Colt .44 revolver. "Let's move, men," he encouraged. "Never know when something can go wrong."

They swung onto the horses—Ty's animal was a leggy sorrel with one white stocking and fire in its eyes, no more than three years old at a guess. They splashed across the wide, shallow river, the horses hoofs kicking up star-silvered fans of water, emerged on the far side of the Gila where another thick willow grove grew, walked their ponies through the undergrowth and out onto open ground.

A wide plain, studded here and there with dry bunch grass, spread out before them, running all the way to the northern hills and south for uncountable miles. Not a single light showed anywhere across the dark land.

"Let's put a few miles between us and the fort, gents," the stubby man said. He heeled his horse's flanks and started forward out onto the long plains, and the deserters followed. By the time the moon rose it was nearly midnight and the horses and men had both had enough of riding for one night. Finding a suitable shelter—only a shallow cave no more than ten feet deep—set among the low hills, their guide held up his hand and swung down from his shuddering horse.

"We'll rest up here," he told them. There was a trickle of water seeping from the walls of the cave, enough to satisfy the horses, and they drank from a depression where the water pooled. Obviously he had not come upon this spot by accident. There were signs of old campfires—burned wood and smoky streaks on the cavern wall, indications that this was a regular stop along the route utilized by deserters.

Ty and Corby sagged to the ground, backs against the stone of the cavern, sipping water from the canteens that had been hung from the pommels of their saddles. The Indian was more active.

"Here, Tamash!" the stocky man said, speaking to the Apache. "What do you think you're doing?"

The Indian was seated on the ground. He had removed his boots and was now tugging his trousers off. The Apache looked up with cold black eyes and answered, "Man said I could go." Tamash tossed his army pants aside. He stood up and began unbuttoning his tunic.

"Nobody told me that," the stout little man said. His hand had lowered to rest on the butt of his holstered revolver. "You better come along with us."

"No," Tamash said firmly. "Man said I could go after I do this one more time."

"What man?"

"Man with no name," Tamash replied. He now threw his tunic aside and stood, wearing only a loincloth of white linen, facing the man with the gun. Tamash proceeded to slip on a pair of doeskin moccasins he had concealed somewhere inside his uniform.

"I think you better ride on with me," the stubby man said threateningly. "I don't want to get into any trouble for letting you run off. Why'd you agree to do this if you weren't wishing to ride with us?"

Tamash explained in passable, but oddly accented English. "I joined the army to scout. Honorable work. Then they made me guard men caged like animals, watching them die, some." Tamash shook his head, "This is not honorable work. The army says I cannot go since I have made my mark on a piece of paper. Now I am gone."

"You're gone when I say you're gone," the man with the gun said. He had drawn his Colt, and as Tamash swung onto his horse's back, he cocked it and raised the muzzle, training it on the Indian.

"*Let him go!*"

The gunhand shifted his eyes in time to see Corby, his eyes wild in a dirt-streaked face, standing with his fists clenched. Ty carefully corked his canteen and placed it aside.

"Sit down, kid," the stubby guide said coolly. His pistol was still trained on Tamash, who sat his pony stoically, his bare chest rising and falling heavily. "I'd hate to shoot you—every man I lose costs me money."

"I said, leave him alone. Let him go!" Corby said, advancing a step.

"Mind your own business," the guide growled. He eyed Corby's thin frame. "You're nothing! You hear me, kid? Little punk growling like a bear." The man laughed out loud and Corby launched himself at him. Ty was quicker and he grabbed Corby's legs before he could reach the man with the gun, and he pulled him down to the floor of the cave. Aimed at nothing, the Colt discharged and a .44 caliber bullet whined off the cavern walls. Tamash saw his chance and he took it. Heeling his horse roughly, he turned its head and raced out of the cave to be swallowed up immediately by the darkness of the desert night.

The man with the gun walked to the entrance to the cave, searched the plains with his eyes and then grunted, holstering his Colt. "Hell with it. Let the rat go." His expression was bitter as he turned to study Corby, still on his face against the cavern floor, Ty sitting on his legs. "You, I owe," he said.

"Leave it alone," Ty said. "As you say, if you lose another man on the trail it comes out of your pay."

"*I* won't leave it alone!" Corby insisted loudly. He writhed beneath Ty's weight, trying to wriggle free.

"You let it go, too," Ty said, placing his hand on Corby's back. "I didn't go through all it took to break you out of the stockade just to have you get yourself shot up."

"You!" Corby said. His eyes were feverish as Ty finally let him sit up and dust himself off. "What did *you* do to break me out, Ty? Tell me. We walked out together. No one was carrying me."

Ty didn't reply. It wasn't worth it. The gunman seemed to have cooled down by now. He had returned his gun to its holster and was now untying a blanket from behind his saddle. "Let's help these horses shed some leather and then turn in, men," he said. "Dawn's not far away and we've got to be riding at first light."

Later, in the nearly complete darkness of the cave, they could hear the guide snoring softly, rolled up in his single blanket. That wasn't the sound that disturbed Ty's own rest. There was movement nearer at hand and opening one eye he saw Corby crouched near him, a fist-sized rock clenched in his hand. Ty grabbed Corby's arm and pulled it aside roughly.

"What the hell are you doing!" he hissed.

"I'm going to kill him," Wynn said. "I can't take any more from men like him."

"Let it go, Wynn."

"No!" He tried to shake Ty's hand away. "I'm going to kill him."

If that were to happen, they would have no way of finding the camp of the Shadow Riders. They would only be
escapees wandering a land they were unfamiliar with, running the risk of being hunted down, shot as deserters or
hung for murder.

Ty told Corby quietly, reasonably, "We have to ride
with him. There's no other way. The army catches us and
you'll be right back on the chain gang again. For a very
long time."

Slowly Ty felt the rage in Corby ebb. He looked steadily
now at Ty. His eyes were not those of the kid Ty had taken
under his wing. They were harder, angrier. Just now his
anger seemed to be concentrated on Ty.

"I thought you were my friend," Corby said. Then his
fingers slowly unclenched and the rock fell free. Corby
turned his back on Ty, rolled up in his own blanket and
pretended to sleep.

The canyon mouth yawned wide before them as they entered the low broken hills. The morning sun still did not
reach into the canyon bottom, nor had it heated it. It was
blessedly cool and dim. A welcome relief from the searing
stretch of badlands they had crossed that morning, riding
slowly and steadily beneath the heated sky over trackless
land where no water was to be found until the horses walked
with their heads down, now and then stumbling. Even Ty's
three-year-old sorrel, young and healthy, had struggled
mightily along the way.

Now the canyon confines closed around them, and they
rode in deep shadow along a rocky, upward-winding trail

carved roughly against the face of the upthrust walls of the gorge. They followed their guide higher, riding in silence. The floor of the canyon was hundreds of feet below them now. The edge of the trail fell off perpendicularly, leaving the horses no room for error. It would be a hell of a road for any pursuing force to try fighting its way up, Ty reflected.

And anyone attempting to follow them would have to fight. Ty had noticed the men . . . spotted about here and there on even higher ground. The trail was closely watched by lookouts.

"How much farther?" Corby muttered, but he wasn't answered. They plodded on, winding their way farther into the craggy highlands. Then, an hour later they emerged from between massive stacks of boulders flanking the trail onto a wide flatland. The grass there was dry and brown, but there was grass, and here and there a gnarled live oak tree. Four or five cottonwood trees could be seen in the near distance, indicating a creek or some sort of water source.

As they crossed the sun-bright valley, Ty saw cattle scattered across the land. The trail beneath them showed signs of many horses having passed recently in both directions. Rounding a shoulder of a bulky, low-topped mesa, they got their first sight of the home ranch, the Shadow Riders' hideout.

The trail followed the contour of the dark mesa, and they rode in shadow again as they approached the scattered buildings of the rough settlement. Two long buildings sat side by side near a grove of oak trees. They resembled nothing more than army barracks—how fitting, Ty thought. Between the barracks was a neat well house.

Beyond these was a corral where dozens of horses stood motionlessly beneath the yellow sun. They were separated into two groups. In one group sorrels, roans, a piebald mare and two black horses munched at their hay without much interest. The other section of the wide corral held twelve or more regulation army bays, all alike in color and height. These had their obvious use. Men disguising themselves as soldiers needed horses that would not give them away. They rode slowly past the barracks where three indolent-appearing men watched them with uncaring eyes from the porch, and proceeded toward another structure, built so close to the mesa that it was still in deep shadow though the sun was high. Long and low, it had been built in the shape of an "L," as if a later addition had been built onto an existing house. The longer section was made of new lumber, still unweathered by the elements, confirming this guess. The house had a porch running its entire width, canopied and newly painted in dark green. The windows were high and narrow, the door massive.

Higher on the mesa, Ty could make out a stone house overlooking the valley. This, he guessed, had been the original rancher's home, built to withstand Indian attacks.

They reined up in front of the wooden house and the little man swung down. Looking across his saddle at Ty and Corby he told them, "You're going to meet some people here. If you're smart you'll answer sharply when you're asked any questions and ask none of your own."

They tied their horses loosely to the hitchrail and stepped up onto the wooden porch. Ty dusted himself off with his hat and stretched saddle-weary back and legs.

Replacing his hat, he turned to study the layout of the out-law ranch as their guide rapped on the heavy plank door. It would be a difficult task for any body of men, no matter how large, to approach the hideout and mount a campaign against the heavily armed men. The Shadow Riders had chosen well. Still, there was always a way if you were de-termined enough, and Ty meant to find it.

The door opened and Ty turned to follow the others into the dark interior of the house.

A man with a Winchester lounged against the doorframe, eyeing them as they entered, looking for weapons. Satisfied, he allowed them to pass and make their way through a sur-prisingly well-furnished drawing room with green velvet-covered chairs and matching settee, with brass andirons and a brass screen before a wide native stone fireplace. The floor was carpeted—another luxury a man seldom saw in this country—and the walls of the corridor they entered were paneled with highly polished oak illuminated by the muted light of two green-glass lanterns. The door at the end of the hallway was open.

The little man took off his hat as they crossed the thresh-old and entered a dark office with a broad carved-oak desk. The carpeting was wine red, and matching drapes hung from floor to ceiling over two windows. The man behind the desk glanced up, closed a book he had been reading and let his dark eyes search their faces.

He was lean, narrow-faced, and cold-eyed. He wore a town suit and a shirt with ruffles showing at the cuffs. A long scar ran from the corner of his right eye to his chin, marring his good looks. His mouth was expressionless; it barely moved when he spoke.

"Where's the other one, Spud?" he asked coldly. "There were supposed to be three."

"One of 'em made a break for it," the man called Spud said nervously. "It was that Indian guard. Wanted to go home."

"You let him go?" the man behind the desk asked as if with idle curiosity.

Spud grew more nervous. There was a sheen of cold sweat on his forehead. "I couldn't stop him. He just jumped his pony and was gone . . . I couldn't chase after him, with these two . . ."

The man behind the desk held up an impatient hand. "I don't need to hear the details. You'll be paid for two men. See Frank about your money."

"Yes, sir," Spud said with immense relief. Ty took Spud's advice and remained silent, only waiting. It was a tense moment. If the man behind the desk had reason to suspect him, the game would be over before it had begun. Now those dark eyes met Ty's directly. It was like looking into the eyes of a rattlesnake. There was no expression at all in them, but much menace.

"Who are you?" he asked.

"Tyrone Cannfield."

He glanced at a sheet of yellow paper on his desk. Apparently he had notes concerning Ty's record scribbled there. "Yes," he said, looking Ty over, "you should fit in here."

The snake eyes flickered to the pale, drawn Corby. "Your name's Corby, right?" Wynn nodded. "I don't know much else about you. What are you doing here?"

"I just sort of came along," Wynn said more boldly than Ty would have expected. "I wouldn't have made it this far if I'd had a chance to finish things."

The scarred man's eyes narrowed. "What do you mean?" he demanded.

"None of us would have made it this far if I hadn't been stopped." He glanced poisonously at Spud. "I intended to bash this gent's head in. Cannfield stopped me or I would have done it."

"Why is that?" the man behind the desk asked. The corner of his mouth twitched with possible amusement.

"I don't like him. I don't like his mouth. He'd have got it on the trail if I'd had a gun."

Spud listened to this outburst with surprise. He opened his mouth to speak, but did not. He had been asked no question by the man with no name. White fingers drummed on the desk top. The dark, unreadable eyes remained fixed on the freckled, pale face of Corby, a face now twisted with bitterness.

"All right. I think you might fit in as well, Corby. As for your murderous thoughts, keep control of them. I have my uses for each of my men, Spud included. They are dispensable only when I decide they are."

Then, without another word, without dismissing them, he opened his book again and began reading.

Spud led them through the house and out into the brilliant sunlight. He mopped his forehead with a red bandana and said, without looking at them, "Go to the nearest bunkhouse and ask for Storch. He'll show you where to put up your horses and grab some grub."

Watching Spud walk away, leading his horse, Ty muttered, "Looks like you put the fear of God into him, Wynn."

The young deserter's voice was cold and determined when he answered, "Fearing God won't do him any good. He'd better start fearing me. I wasn't just talking, Ty. I will take no more from any man. That's been decided. My own weakness made my life miserable back there. I'll not take any slight from any man. As for Spud—I *will* kill him if I get the chance, just like I'll kill any man who scorns me again."

Then, without waiting for Ty to follow, Corby started off toward the bunkhouse, limping heavily. The knee Lieutenant Deveraux had kicked was still bothering him and probably always would. Ty watched him go, wondering if he should have left Wynn behind and wondering what sort of monster he had helped create.

Chapter Four

"Wake up and roll out!"

It was totally dark, cold and eerily still in the bunkhouse when Ty was shaken awake by the dour camp boss, Arnie Storch. Ty sat up, stretching. Corby had already been awakened. The young deserter was standing before a starlit window, slipping his suspenders over his shoulders. Ty dressed unhurriedly in the new clothes and boots Storch had given them the day before, and walked the length of the barracks, passing through into the dining area where the smell of boiling coffee lifted his sprits. The room was much warmer than the bunkhouse. Fires burned brightly in the twin iron stoves as the silent Mexican cook prepared breakfast.

Storch stood, hands on hips, looking out the dark eastern window. Hatless and frowning, the camp foreman seemed lost in thought. He was, however, only calculating the morning's duties.

44

"You two finish your coffee. Then get to work mucking out the stables. See that there's new hay in the corral troughs and that the ponies have fresh water."

"Why us?" Corby asked sullenly. His face was morose, dark with lingering anger. Storch turned to face him, his pocked face stern.

"New meat always takes care of the chores."

"Worse than the army," Corby complained, stirring a spoonful of sugar into his coffee.

"Not hardly," Storch answered. "By the time the week is out you'll already have made more than a month in the army would pay. And," he added, "no one is going to throw you into irons here."

Noticing the new Colt revolver holstered high on Storch's hip, Corby went on, "We haven't been issued weapons yet. What good would we be in a fight?"

"You'll get what you need when you need it," Storch said. His tone indicated that he had already taken a dislike to Corby. "For now, you do what I say. I'm in charge for the time being."

Corby was poor company on this morning, and so taking his coffee cup with him, Ty moved out onto the porch in front of the bunkhouse. He stood watching the silent pre-dawn sky. It was too early for the morning birds. The camp was unlighted. No one was moving yet. A broad-winged owl cut a dark silhouette as it winged past heading for its day-time roost. The morning was cool but windless. Steam rose from Ty's coffee cup. He leaned against a pole and considered what he must do.

Getting the layout of the place fixed firmly in his mind

would be no problem. He needed to count heads, estimate how many outlaws any attacking force might expect to encounter. Were there other Shadow Riders now absent from the camp, perhaps out raiding somewhere?

Several other questions presented themselves. Who, for example, was the man with no name, the leader of the gang? An ex-soldier himself? He seemed to have a slight southern accent. He probably hailed from one of the border states. Was he, perhaps, an ex-Confederate who could not admit that the war was long lost? A Quantrill-type raider? It seemed more likely he was in this simply for the plunder.

One other matter Ty wanted to take care of was contacting "Bert" who was supposed to have some method of communicating with the authorities in Phoenix. There was no way of knowing if the informer was still here, had fled or been found out and killed. There was always the possibility that there was more than one man called Bert on the ranch. That would have to be kept in mind before Ty even considered approaching anyone on the subject. The door behind Ty was swung open. A rectangle of lamplight painted itself across the porch planks.

"Time to get with it," Storch said. Ty nodded and with Corby in tow the three walked across the dark yard to the stables. Storch lit a lantern hanging on the wall near the double doors to the building, showed the two ex-soldiers where the tools were, pointed out the hayloft and returned to his own work as the first hint of watery color tinged the eastern sky. Ty and a silently brooding Corby got to work.

By mid-morning the sky had brightened prettily. Birds chittered in the surrounding oak grove and a pleasant breeze had arisen. Outlaws came and went singly, in pairs, and in groups to claim their mounts, saddle and ride away toward the mountain trail.

Corby was nowhere to be found when Ty ambled over toward the corral, his chores completed. That suited Ty well enough; the young trooper was beginning to present a problem and Ty needed no new complications to interfere with his work.

The camp wrangler, Tully, a saturnine man of middle years with a badly bent arm from some accident which had left it broken and not set properly, was perched on the rails of the corral, watching the horses lazing in the afternoon sunshine.

"Mornin'," Ty said, walking up beside the wrangler to rest his folded arms on the top rail, studying the horses himself.

"Fresh meat?" Tully asked without so much as glancing at Ty.

"As fresh as it gets," Ty answered with a smile. "Got in yesterday."

"Things are all right here," Tully said. "Just don't cause no trouble.

"Don't intend to," Ty replied.

"Does it seem to you that the chestnut over there is favoring his right front leg?" Tully asked, pointing at a tall, dark brown pony with a white blaze.

"Could be," Ty said after a moment's consideration. "Could be a bowed tendon. I'd feel that leg for heat."

Tully nodded, his eyes still fixed on the chestnut gelding. "I think he's favoring it," he said.

It was apparent that Tully's life revolved around these horses, and only them. It also seemed to Ty that the man was not too bright. He decided to ask casually, "Know a man up here called Bert?"

Tully's eyes flickered toward Ty's. The look reminded him that a man was not encouraged to ask any questions at all in this camp.

"I just ask because he's a friend of mine. We both rode with General Crook back when the White Mountain trouble was going on. I'd heard he gave himself an early discharge," Ty said with another smile. "Thought he might have wound up here."

"Don't know him. I'd better see to that chestnut," Tully said, leaping agilely down from the corral fence to make his way through the milling herd, slapping a horse or two on the rump in passing.

Ty shook his head. Oh, well, what did he expect? Nothing was going to be easy among the outlaws. He turned to start toward the barracks, intending to mooch another cup of coffee from the cook. He had taken one step when the gunfire began.

Ty spun in the direction of the oak grove, searching for the source of the shots. Storch was racing across the dusty yard, his pistol in hand. Two other men were following, hatless, their own guns drawn. From around the corner of the southern barracks a surrey appeared. Holding the reins, whipping a team of matched white horses forward came the boss himself, the man with no name, dressed in a black suit, wearing a flat-crowned black hat. At his side was a pretty young woman in yellow holding a yellow parasol. The sur-

rey flashed past Ty, the near horse's hoofs barely missing
his boot toes. Ty started out after them at a dead run. Storch
and the two other outlaws were nearly on his heels.

Ty darted through the mottled shade of the oaks and
found where the carriage had halted, on the bank of a dry
gravel-strewn creekbed. The outlaw leader had not gotten
down from the buggy. His scarred face was an expressionless mask. From behind Ty now, Storch and his companions burst from the trees, drawn pistols at the ready as they
charged toward the sandy river bottom. And surrounded
Corby.

Wynn showed neither fear, nor any truculence. When
asked, he handed the pistol he had been using over to
Storch without delay.

"What in hell are you doing?" Storch demanded.
"Where'd you get the gun, anyway?"

"Found it hanging in the tack room. Somebody's spare,
I guess. I decided to get some shooting practice in, since
there was nothing else to do."

"You know you're not supposed to have it!" Storch
said. He turned worriedly toward the outlaw leader. "I told
him he wasn't supposed to have a gun yet."

"I needed the practice," Corby said steadily. "I don't
want to find I've gotten rusty when the time comes that
I need to shoot."

Storch, still obviously upset, worried that he was going
to be blamed for this violation of the rules, stood almost
trembling before the gaze of his boss. The man with no
name smiled—if that was what his habitual twitch at one
corner of his mouth could be called. The infraction seemed

of no concern to him at all. Studying the fixed expression on Corby's face, the outlaw leader said, "Let him keep it, Storch. He's just target shooting. Maybe he's getting ready for Spud."

Ty frowned in disbelief. If the outlaw wasn't encouraging Wynn to commit murder, he was certainly dong nothing to discourage it. Stunned, Storch handed the revolver back to Corby who slid it into his borrowed holster. The outlaw leader had backed the team of white horses and now he turned the carriage away from the streambed, guiding it easily through the grove of old oak trees.

The lady in the yellow dress glanced once at Ty, her blue eyes direct and mocking. Ty turned slowly to watch them go, disappearing into the shadows.

Storch was beside him. The dour camp foreman said, "Remember what you were told about asking questions around here? It goes double for looking at that woman— for so much as thinking about her." The warning given, Storch started back toward the camp, and his two companions followed. Ty glanced at Corby, capturing a smug look of satisfaction on his face. Wynn, it seemed, considered himself to be making rapid progress, already to have found favor with the boss. Ty said nothing to Corby. There was no point in trying to persuade him that he had very likely taken a dangerous step, one that could lead to his own death.

Ty returned to the corral, finding Tully, unconcerned by the activity around him, still tending to the chestnut horse. The wrangler had only one mission in life, one reality, his horses. Nothing else intruded on his small, simple world. Perhaps, Ty thought, Tully was the smartest man in camp.

Ty had been warned to not even think about the blond woman he had seen in the buggy. How could he not? Who in hell was she? Where had she come from? Did she live with the leader of the Shadow Riders? Was she a business partner? A relative? There were too many possibilities. Ty only knew that she was striking, composed, with blue eyes that could melt a man if he let them.

And impossible not to think about.

"Cannfield!" Storch shouted across the yard, and Ty turned that way. "They need help pushing some cattle. Grab yourself a horse and get out there." Storch was pointing toward the eastern end of the mountain valley. He seemed to be in too much of a hurry to give more detailed directions. Ty shrugged and went to saddle his sorrel. How hard could it be to find a herd of cattle?

It was, however, curious to Ty that there would even be cattle up here. Where had they come from? The Shadow Riders, striking hard and fast, always on the run from the law or the army, certainly would not stoop to rustling. Not that they would have any scruples about it, but you can't flee a pursuing posse while you're trying to push a slow-moving herd of stolen cattle ahead of you.

Nor could he imagine trying to drive cattle up the rugged canyon trail they had followed to the high valley. That indicated two things: the cattle were not stolen beeves . . . and there was probably another route out of the valley if you knew where to look. Tightening his cinches, Ty swung aboard the leggy sorrel and started out to the east, watching for dust in the air to indicate the presence of the herd.

With the eager pony moving lightly under him, the barracks now out of view, he felt free. It would have been a pleasure just to ride aimlessly all day. A touch of regret flitted across Ty's thoughts as he considered that it might be a long, long time before he was ever truly free again. He brushed the troublesome thought aside and continued on, slowing the sorrel to a walk—no one had said he had to hurry to reach the herd.

The land ahead was flat, dry grass country. To the north the dark hills crowded the skyline. To the south chaparral grew thickly nearer the long, low mesa. Greasewood, sumac, sage and mesquite knotted together to form a heavy thicket.

Glancing in that direction, Ty saw, or thought he saw, a thin veil of dust rising, rapidly dispersed by the gusting breeze. Cattle? Couldn't be. Maybe a few strays lost in the thicket. If so he should haze them out and head them back toward the main herd. He started that way, following a game trail through the brush which was head-high to a horse with here and there tall thorny mesquite pushing their spiked heads ten feet or more higher.

Pressed in by chaparral on all sides, Ty stopped to listen. Sweat dripped off his forehead and slithered down his spine. The breeze did not penetrate the heavy growth. Nothing stirred but annoying clouds of gnats. Nothing moved. There was no sound.

And then there was. Faint, unidentifiable. Ty let the sorrel walk on, deeper into the thicket, mesquite thorns and clumps of nopal cactus brushing his legs. He heard the sound again, this time much nearer.

This time he could identify the sound. It was a human voice, muffled and weak. Ty urged the sorrel on more quickly.

Now the single word could be understood: "Help." The voice seemed fainter as it reached Ty again, and he wondered if he was riding in the wrong direction. Then a corridor through the thicket opened up in front of him and he emerged onto a sandy flat spreading itself across the land to the very base of the dark mesa.

And there he found her.

It was a woman who had been calling out. She lay against the sand, pressed beneath the weight of a dead black horse, its eye open in startled surprise. Ty swung down before his sorrel had come to a full halt and went to the woman—a girl really—and her wide brown eyes looked up hopefully.

"Fool horse stepped in a squirrel hole . . . rolled. Neck broken," she said breathlessly. Eighteen or nineteen years of age, she was small, her dark hair shorn raggedly. She was wearing a white blouse and men's black jeans. Both of her legs were trapped under the fallen horse, and Ty could see there was no way of pulling her out from under its weight.

"Do something!" the girl pleaded urgently.

"Are your legs broken?"

"I don't think so—I can't feel them at all, actually."

"How did you . . . ?" Ty asked, crouching beside her.

"I kicked out of the stirrups. Tried to jump free. I didn't make it," she added with a pained smile.

"I'm going to try to pull the horse off you," Ty told her. "That's why I asked if your legs were broken. If they are . . ."

"I know!" the girl said, managing to laugh again. She tossed her head so that the dark fringe of hair bounced. "It would hurt. Hurt plenty, but mister, if you don't get it off, I'll be worse than hurt before long."

Ty returned to the sorrel and took his lasso from its saddle tie. He formed a loop as he returned to the fallen black. Straddling the neck, he was able, with some effort to work the noose over muzzle and head and tighten it down. He glanced at the girl who was sitting propped, arms behind her, watching him with interest. Her face was pale; she was trembling, but she showed no sign of panic.

Ty went back to the sorrel and looped the rope around his pommel with a dally knot. He hadn't had the horse long enough to know if it knew how to back off, but either through past training or a dislike of being so near to the dead animal, it started away under Ty's urging. The rope went taut and the black's head lifted, but only briefly. The sorrel did not like this work.

"Try it again!" the girl shouted unhelpfully.

Again Ty backed the unwilling sorrel horse, and this time when the rope drew taut, he heeled the pony. Startled, the sorrel continued in the direction it had been going and the thousand-pound bulk of the black horse slid in a slow arc away from the girl's legs, freeing her.

Grinning, Ty patted the sorrel's neck, threw off the dally and returned to the girl. She was trying to rise, but her legs were numb. Ty went behind her, hooked his hands under her arms and hoisted. The girl gave an involuntary cry of pain.

From the thicket a man on a gray horse appeared, crashing through the chaparral into the clearing. He had a rifle in his hands and he threw it to his shoulder, firing a shot which whipped near Ty's head and sang off into the distance.

"*Let go of her!*" the stranger shouted and he levered a fresh round into the breech of his Winchester. Ty could do nothing but drop the girl and roll to one side. A second rifle shot dug a furrow in the sand, inches from Ty's shoulder and he scurried on hands and knees into the dense thicket, a third shot following, clipping brush near his head in passing.

"Stop it, Judd!" the girl cried. "*Stop!*" She tried to rise to snatch the Winchester from the man's hands, but was unable to. She fell back with a grunt and the big man fired again, wildly.

Ty was not where his attacker had presumed him to be. Moving now in a low crouch to stay below the thicket, Ty moved at run, circling the clearing. His boots made only whispers against the sandy soil, and though the going was tough, he made little noise. He found himself behind the man now, and he squatted down, trying to quiet his ragged breathing. He watched the man—bald, he now saw as he removed his hat and hung it on his saddlehorn, broad-shouldered and big with some flab around his waist. He was walking to where the girl still sat, her head hanging, but his gaze was on the brush beyond where he believed Ty to be hiding.

"I'll just take care of business first," the rifleman told the girl. "Then I'll get you home."

That did it. The man meant to track him down and kill him. And there was a chance that he could do it, now that Ty was afoot. Slowly Ty rose, eased forward so that the hunting man was no more than thirty feet away from him across the open clearing. Crouching himself now, the big man was peering into the thicket, his head cocked to one side as if listening intently.

As Ty stepped from the thicket, the girl's eyes lifted and her lips parted, but she said nothing.

Ty rushed forward across the sandy earth. The rifleman did not hear him coming until Ty had leaped the fallen black horse and hurtled himself through the air at him. Then the big man turned and tried to rise, his eyes wide. He attempted to bring his rifle to bear, but Ty's shoulder thudded against his chest and he went sprawling, the Winchester discharging into the air.

The rifle flew free of his grip as Ty slammed into him and together they hit the ground, the big man landing on his back. The breath was driven roughly from his lungs and a small croak rose from his throat. He tired to lift his arms to fight back, but Ty had already driven a solid right fist which landed on the hinge of the big man's jaw and his head lolled back.

Ty lifted his arm to deliver a second blow into his attacker's face, but held back. The big man was out cold, eyelids fluttering, mouth hanging open. Ty stood shakily, wiping the hair back from his eyes. He glanced at the girl and met her eyes which showed no expression but consternation.

"You're a big help," she muttered. "The both of you."

Ty smiled fleetingly. Snatching up the Winchester from the sand he went to her and asked, "Can you stand up?"

"I don't know—nobody's given me the chance to find out yet." She glanced at the motionless man. "One punch, huh? Judd won't live that down. You must have a kick like a mule."

"Pure luck," Ty said. He placed the rifle down and asked her, "Shall we give it a try, then?"

"I don't intend to sit here all day," the girl answered. Ty saw a hint of fear in her wide brown eyes. Perhaps she was thinking that she might not be able to stand at all, that the weight of the horse falling across her legs might have done more damage than she was yet aware of.

Ty again stepped behind her and placed his hands under her arms. "Let's see how this goes," he said. "How do your legs feel now?"

"Tingly."

"That's a good sign, I think. Circulation getting back to normal."

He wasn't sure of that, but it did no harm to offer positive thoughts to her. There was only one way to find out how severe the damage was and so he lifted her surprisingly light weight until she managed to plant her boots firmly on the ground. Ty felt her sag in his arms.

"Hurt?" he asked.

"No, but they don't seem to be supporting me like normal."

"All right, then." Ty looked around. The man, Judd, was twitching his feet and hands. Some muttered sounds bubbled from his lips. "Let's get you aboard his horse and I'll take you home."

"No!" she said in sheer panic. "You can't!" She managed to turn in his arms and now stood looking up at him with terrified eyes. Her fingers clutched at the front of his blood-red shirt.

"Why not?" Ty asked.

"It's not allowed. If you don't know . . . nobody can go near."

"No? Well I am," Ty said sternly. "You've got to get home."

"What about Judd?" she asked in a small voice.

"He's not ready to ride yet," Ty said.

"I mean . . . how is he going to get home if I take his horse?"

"Let him walk. Maybe that'll give him time to consider what he's done. Come on," Ty said roughly, "let's get you up and get going."

Ty boosted the girl onto the gray horse's back and swung aboard the sorrel. "Lead on," he said cheerfully, and she started Judd's horse away from the clearing, looking back to see the big bald man siting up now, rubbing his head, watching them with dismal eyes.

"He'll be in a lot of trouble," the girl said as they rode toward the shoulder of the dark mesa.

"Good," Ty replied, still bitter about being shot at for his good intentions. "Where are we going?"

"Up there," she answered, lifting her eyes to the barely visible stone house Ty had seen earlier. The granite building sat like a fortress three hundred feet or so up the flank of the mesa. Strong-appearing, forbidding, it seemed an unlikely place for a pretty young girl to live.

He rode on in silence. Ty kept an eye on her, watching for any sign that she might weaken and slump from the saddle. He also kept an eye on the trail behind them. No matter that he now carried Judd's Winchester across his saddle, Ty could not be sure that the big man would not find a way to follow them, and Judd might not have been alone.

The switchback trail up the side of the mesa was no wider than the canyon trail, and steeper. They rode in shadow, but the day had grown warm, and there was little relief from the heat. Slowly they climbed, the horses moving easily, plodding their way upward. Now and then the dark-haired girl glanced back at Ty with those wide brown eyes of hers, and he could see the uneasiness in them.

Ty didn't like things much himself, but what was he to do—leave the girl where she lay? And so he rode on following her. Below he could see most of the long valley: the outlaw camp, the tiny figures of a distant cattle herd to the east, the crumpled brown hills surrounding the flat.

The girl on the gray horse was in front of him, and then she was not. She had just disappeared. Puzzled, Ty followed, until he found the cut in the granite walls of the mesa. The chute, no more than thirty feet long, led from the trail up onto the crescent-shaped hillside ledge where the stone house stood in its splendid isolation far above the world below. Ty followed the girl's lead and walked his sorrel to the hitching post set at the side of the house which was shaded by twin cottonwood trees. Swinging down from his saddle, he heard the footsteps before he saw the old man step from behind the corner of the house, shotgun leveled. "Move, mister," a determined voice said, "and I'll cut you in half."

Chapter Five

T y's eyes slid toward the man with the shotgun, not liking what he saw. He was careful to make no move that might be misinterpreted.

"Throw down that rifle!" a booming voice ordered. "And stand away from my niece." Ty did as he was told and stood watching, hands in the air as the gray-bearded man with the wind-tangled hair took another step forward. He was wearing a deep scowl. Both of the hammers on his double-twelve shotgun were eared back, ready to be dropped.

"Are you all right, Bobbi?" the old man asked with concern, keeping his gaze fixed on the tall stranger.

"Mostly," she answered. "Old Dancer took a tumble. Broke his neck. I was pinned under him. This man got me out from under and brought me up here."

"You know better than to bring anyone up here," the old man said gruffly.

"She didn't have any choice," Ty said. The old man was listening to no further explanation.

"Where's Judd? I sent him looking for you."

Bobbi answered, "Judd misunderstood matters and tried to shoot this man. There was a fight, and . . ."

"You killed Judd!" the old man said, his fierce eyes growing wilder. Bobbi soothed him slightly.

"It was only a fist fight, Uncle Morgan! Judd got knocked out; he's all right."

"None of this should have happened," Morgan said angrily, running his fingers through his shaggy gray hair. "You know better than to ride off alone, Bobbi! Judd knows better than to go shoot without good cause. You"—he spat at Ty—"you should know better than to come near this house. It's off-limits to all of you. What are you doing on the east end of the valley anyway?"

"They sent for someone to help with the cattle," Ty said, "I was the nearest man. The rest was pure accident."

"Those are *my* cattle," Morgan said hotly. "Our cattle," he amended, glancing at the girl. A frown drew his heavy eyebrows together. "Bobbi, why are you still sitting your horse? Swing down."

Bobbi's smile was faint. "I'm not sure I can make it, Uncle Morgan. I tried to explain to you what happened. My legs are hurt pretty bad."

"Broke?" the old man asked with sudden anxiety.

"I don't think so," Bobbi answered, with a bigger smile which was still less than cheering. Pain lingered around the corners of her mouth.

"Then . . ." The old man looked suddenly flustered. His

shotgun muzzle, however, never wavered. If he ever cut loose with it, Ty knew he would be blown in two. Morgan considered deeply, but swiftly. "All right," he said, making his decision. "Help her down, young man. You'll have to carry her into the house, it seems."

Under the gaze of the glowering uncle, Ty helped Bobbi slide from the saddle and into his arms. Turning, he started toward the front of the house, Morgan and his shotgun trailing. A gusting wind now whipped across the mesa. Brooding dark clouds made their slow ominous way across the skies, casting shadows. The temperature was falling rapidly. Ty wondered if it was going to rain. It seemed unlikely at this time of year, but occasional, brief thunderstorms had been known to hit the high desert without warning.

The front door to the stone house, constructed of heavy planks bound with iron straps, stood open, and Ty ducked inside, Bobbi in his arms, her slender arms around his neck. The interior of the living room was low-ceilinged, dominated by a huge fireplace. Striped Navajo Indian rugs were scattered across the floor and hung on the stone walls by way of decoration. Three leather-bottomed chairs, turned to face the fireplace, completed the furnishings.

"Which way?" Ty asked his unwilling host.

"Through there," Morgan growled, reluctant it seemed, to invite Ty deeper into the house, especially to cross the threshold into what appeared to be Bobbi's bedroom. A multicolored quilt covered a low, narrow bed. A dresser with attached oval mirror and a straight-backed wooden chair were the only other items there.

Ty gently placed Bobbi down on her bed, pulled the pillow out from beneath the quilt and tucked it under her head. She looked up gratefully, her hand lingering briefly on his arm.

Morgan noticed this and said in his usual snarling voice, "You can get going now, traitor."

At the word Ty turned in surprise. "Traitor?" he asked in a low voice.

"That's right! What else do you call a man who breaks his promise to his country and runs for the hills when there's the threat of having to do something he doesn't feel like doing? Traitors and cowards, the bunch of you," Morgan went on. "Scared to face a real fighting man, like an Apache warrior, willing to pillage and loot the countryside when only honest, hard-working family men are going to be encountered."

"If you feel that way . . ." Ty started to ask in some confusion, but he was interrupted.

"There you are!" Judd shouted.

He stood facing Ty, hatless, dusty, perspiring heavily, his shirt torn by brambles, his jaw swollen.

"I'll take you apart!" He had recovered his Winchester rifle which Ty had been forced to drop outside. He seemed ready to use it again. The bald man ground one row of teeth against the other as he hovered in the doorway, glaring at Ty.

"Forget it, Judd!" Morgan ordered. "There's been enough excitement for one day. He's just leaving. Let him go."

"Thank you," Bobbi said from her bed, offering Ty a weak, sincere smile.

"You're welcome. I think you'll be up and about by morning, Bobbi. Probably you just have a few deep bruises, maybe a stretched ligament or two."

"Nobody asked for your medical opinion," Morgan said. "I said that it's time for you to get going."

Ty rode down the switchback trail slowly, his eyes lifting now and then to the clouds along the northern horizon which had begun to stack themselves into dark menacing thunderheads. The wind was brisker, the temperature still falling. He could see no one else, nothing, moving across the long valley. From the trail above he was able to spot an easier way around the dense thicket and he rode that way, aiming for the home camp as distant thunder rumbled.

This day had presented no new strategies for thwarting the Shadow Riders. He did not, as of now, see any way possible to complete his mission satisfactorily. But many new, probably irrelevant puzzles had cropped up. Who, for example, was the blond lady in the carriage? Who was Morgan, and why, if he hated the Shadow Riders as he claimed, would he share his range with them? Was there another way out of the long valley? Ty wished that he had been able to ride as far as the cattle herd. There might have been some indication of another, hidden trail at the east end of the ranch. He rode on gloomily. The clouds lowered and the land darkened. He saw the fizzle of lightning in the far distance, above the broken hills, followed by the muffled rumble of thunder. He bowed his head to the wind and rode on. The first large splatters of rain began to pock the dusty earth just as he reached the home ranch, led his sorrel into the stable and unsaddled.

Making his way toward the barracks, he could see that the other bunkhouse was also lighted, and the silhouettes of many men moving about within. Smoke rose from its kitchen's iron chimney. Inside his own bunkhouse he came upon more men, twenty to thirty of them at least, drinking coffee or whiskey. These were whiskered, trail-dusty men, all armed with a belt gun. The absent raiders had returned to camp, perhaps driven home by the arriving storm.

Ty passed Storch who only nodded to him, and walked to his bunk where he tossed his hat onto a bedpost before stretching out, studying the ceiling as men caroused roughly around him. Above the tumult a familiar voice rose, and Ty looked toward the kitchen end of the barracks to see Corby standing, tin cup in his hand, entertaining a knot of tough outlaws.

"You serious?" someone asked and Corby answered passionately.

"You'd better believe I'm serious—the man did me wrong. The next time I run across Spud, there's going to be gunplay."

A few of the Shadow Riders laughed out loud at the thin recruit's vow. Ty frowned, knowing that any hint of mockery would only goad Corby on. He had made his boast; now there was no backing down from it in front of the rough outlaws. Not if he was ever to be accepted as a man among men.

"Boss won't like it," another outlaw said and Corby laughed.

"You're wrong! He knows the situation. He gave me the go-ahead."

Which, Ty knew, was an exaggeration, but not much of one. The man with no name did indeed know what Corby had been planning, and for his own reasons had said nothing at all to shut it down.

"Spud's not so bad," someone in the group said.

That raised Corby's rant to new heights. "He's yellow. A spineless, back-shooting snake!" Corby shouted. "I'll show you what he's made of the next time our paths cross."

At that moment, Spud entered the barracks, damp with rain. He flicked the water from his hat and looked around, half-smiling. "What's going on, boys? Did I miss something?"

"You didn't miss a thing," Corby said, stepping forward. His words were now obviously slurred by liquor. The outlaws parted, making a path for Corby. No hand reached out to stop him. No one said a word; it had gone too far. Corby had made his boast.

"Why don't you and I step outside for a minute, Spud," Corby said in a low voice. Ty rose from his bunk and started that way, but he was blocked by the bodies of a dozen men.

"I don't know . . . What do you want, Corby?" Spud asked in an anxious voice which he tried to turn into a menacing tone. Corby was determined to make his play and he grinned. It was a vicious expression Ty never would have expected to see on the face of the young soldier. Propped up by liquor, encouraged by the silent eyes of the watching outlaws, Corby could not back down now. Not without suffering the mockery of the other men.

"Wynn!" Ty called out. "Let it go." Corby ignored Ty. His attention was fixed only on Spud whose lower lip had begun to tremble though his eyes remained hostile.

"I'm asking you to step outside with me, Spud," Corby said again. "Will you do it or are you as yellow as I've been telling everybody?"

"Well, damn you!" Spud said in exasperation. "What do you want to do this to me for? You little punk! I should . . ."

"Here's your chance," Corby said. "The time for talking your game is over. Step outside."

Spud angrily spun on his heel and started for the door. He, too, was bound by the code he lived by. To refuse Corby's challenge could only result in humiliation and a life more painful than getting shot. He did not look back. The door swung open and Corby followed confidently after him. Outside the rain was falling in a thin veil. It dripped from the eaves of the bunkhouse and a cold wind was gusting, drifting some of the rain inside. Ty tried to make his way to the door, but everyone was now crowded near it and he had not reached it before he heard the roar of two closely spaced gunshots.

Corby returned, alone. Someone slapped him on the back and Corby grinned. He was handed another cup of whiskey which he set aside as he thumbed two empty cartridges from his Colt. *Two.* That meant that Spud had not managed to get a shot off. Perhaps it meant that Wynn had simply gunned the man down.

Feeling slightly sick—not at the thought of death in itself, but at the thought of what Wynn Corby had become—Ty returned to his bunk, closed his eyes and listened to the loud congratulations and the retelling of what had happened. Corby was one of them now. He had become a man at last.

And a killer.

Daylight was startlingly bright, sun-spray shafting through the broken clouds and damp oak trees. Ty was the only man awake in the bunkhouse as he made his way to the kitchen and asked the cook for coffee. Storch was seated at the table. The red-headed camp boss scratched his pocked cheek as he used a stubby pencil to laboriously total his supplies.

Storch looked up at Ty and nodded. The camp boss asked nothing about yesterday's work assignment. Ty had the idea he had been sent over to the cattle herd simply because he was standing idle and Arnie thought that might look bad for him.

Stepping outside into the fresh morning air, Ty looked at the spot where the gunfight must have occurred. There was no dead man to be seen. Curious, Ty stepped off the porch and moved around a little. Now he saw bootprints imprinted in the damp earth and the twin grooves which might have been left by a man's feet as he was dragged away.

The mystery resolved itself as a youngish, lanky, blond-haired man walked around the corner of the bunkhouse, a shovel over his shoulder. He grinned and nodded to Ty who noticed that the kid was not wearing a gun. Fresh meat. Thankful that he had not been given the job of burying Spud himself, Ty nodded in return. The man with the shovel came up to where he stood sipping at his steaming coffee.

"Where are you in from?" he asked.

Ty smiled in return and answered, "Didn't they explain rule number one to you? Don't ask any questions."

"Oh," the narrow man said, scratching his head as he leaned on his shovel. "Sorry. It's just habit. I'm a friendly guy. Mind if I at least ask your handle?"

"Ty."

"Bill Cox," the newcomer said, thrusting out a red big-knuckled hand. "I didn't realize they were really that touchy about matters. Is that what happened to . . . ?" he asked, nodding his head in the general direction of the grave he had just finished digging for Spud.

"That's another question, isn't it?" Ty asked, but he grinned as he said it. It was difficult not to like the amiable Cox at first sight, but Ty forced himself to remember that every man here was a criminal to some extent or the other. It might be that Cox was the kind who could smile as he gunned a man down. At any rate, Ty could not afford any close relationships. The last friendship he had formed had only brought him grief.

It rained most of the next day and the bored men slept or stood sullenly around the bunkhouse. Card games were begun and a lot of raw whiskey was drunk. The lanterns were doused early and the grumbling, restless outlaws turned in to exchange a few rough jokes before subsiding into a tournament of lusty snoring.

Dawn the following day was a colorful flare across the western sky, bleeding into the high windows of the barracks when Ty was awakened by a sharp slap to his face. He pawed his way awake and discovered a man in a striped shirt and a hat with a silver band standing over him. He wore a Colt low on his right hip and had the air of authority about him.

"Get up. We're riding," the man said, and fuzzily Ty nodded and sat up. He had to untangle the leather from his face, for the slap that had awakened him had been caused by a gunbelt being tossed at Ty.

The man with the silver hat band crossed the bunkhouse and shook Corby awake as well. Ty winced inwardly. Wherever he was bound, he would have preferred to travel without the company of Corby. Other men, half-asleep or half-drunk opened red eyes and peered at Ty as he stood, dressed and strapped on his Colt, checking its loads. Seeing that it was not a general call, they tugged up their blankets and went back to sleep.

Ty walked toward the kitchen and its welcome warmth. Only the cook was there and he served Ty coffee without being asked. Sunlight brightened, and the fire faded from the dawn sky as Ty sat drinking his coffee. Corby came in, glanced at Ty, startled it seemed, and took a seat as far away from Ty as possible.

The rear door slammed open and Cox entered with an

armful of firewood which he dumped beside the cookstoves. Cox nodded to Ty as he stacked the wood. Behind him Storch came in, wearing rubber overshoes.

"Get yourself a pair of these from the barn," Storch told Cox, indicating his footwear. "It's still plenty muddy around here." He removed his sheepskin jacket and hung it on a peg.

"I see Champ got you up," the camp boss said to Ty. He nodded, indicating the sidearm Ty now wore.

"Champ?" Ty said.

"Champ Studdard. He's one of the field commanders," Storch told him. Make sure you're saddled and ready to go when he wants you. Champ's an impatient man."

While talking, Storch had poured himself a cup of coffee. He now sat down opposite Ty and motioned to Cox to help himself to a cup. Corby stared silently into his own coffee mug, turning it slowly. Now he lifted his eyes, and addressing Storch, asked, "What's up? No one's talking to me this morning?"

Cox glanced at Corby; Storch continued to ignore him. Wynn got up from the table, nearly tipping his chair over and stormed out the front door, leaving it open to the chill of the morning wind. Cox rose and closed it, returning to the table to finish his coffee. He looked questioningly at Ty but got no response.

When Ty went out into the yard the sun was just raising itself above the crowns of the oak trees. The wind was fresh but not strong. The upper limits of the branches swayed gently; a few low clouds, white and thin, lazed past. Ty rounded

the corner of the barracks and walked to the stable, his boots
leaving impressions in the reddish mud. No one was in the
dark barn. It seemed there was to be little activity today.
Saddling his sorrel, Ty led it out and around to the front of
the barracks, heeding Storch's warning to be ready the instant Studdard was ready to ride.

When Corby finally appeared to join Ty, he remained
seated on his dun pony, hat tugged down to hide his eyes in
shadow. No words were exchanged while they waited for
Champ. Ty felt a pang of sorrow over the loss of his friend,
but there was nothing to be done about it. A man who would
murder only to gain status was only to be despised. Ty did
miss the other Corby, the uncertain kid he had first met, but
that Corby seemed to have lost his way out in the long
desert.

Studdard approached them sitting his deep-chested blue
roan easily. Sunlight glittered off the silver conchoes deco-
rating his bridle and saddle and the silver hatband he wore.
Besides the Colt .44 he was armed with, Champ Studdard
carried twin forward-facing rifles on either side of his saddle. Oddly, the walnut stocks of these Winchester '73s were
studded with brass tack decoration as Indians were fond of
doing. Probably there were spare pistols in Champ's saddlebags. One thing was sure, the Shadow Rider did not intend
to be outgunned wherever he was riding.

"Ready?" was all Champ said. Nodding his head he
started away, jerking his roan's head around sharply, heeling
it hard. Before they had exited the yard, though, a man ran
toward them from the big house hailing them, waving his

arm frantically. Ty had seen him once before, a swarthy man they called Tavares. He was some sort of distant relative of the Mexican cook. Champ reined in with disgust and waited for Tavares to reach them.

"Boss, he say," Tavares, out of breath panted, "you wait and take Miss Dahlia home."

"How much time am I supposed to have?" Champ said angrily. Under his breath, he added, "Now I'm a nurse-maid."

But even Studdard wasn't about to buck the boss's orders. They started their horses toward the big house where the twin white horses stood hitched to the buggy. At the hitch rail stood a stubby little paint pony. Before they had reached the house, the boss appeared, dressed in a dark green suit, his hair parted in the middle, slicked down. On his arm was the lady in yellow—Miss Dahlia. She wore fawn driving gloves reaching nearly to her elbows. She was escorted to the buggy and helped up. Placing the furled parasol beside her, she unwound the reins from the brake handle as if she knew what she was doing.

As Ty watched, another woman appeared, emerging from the house on stiff legs, her face decorated with a wide smile. She went to the carriage and whispered a few words to Dahlia, holding one of her hands briefly.

Then she walked to the paint pony and swung aboard. Waving, she turned the pony and rode away at an easy canter. Ty knew her.

Bobbi.

"What is she doing here?" Ty muttered out loud. Champ

glanced at him sharply and said: "She's got a right. Dahlia's her sister, isn't she?"

She was? Ty stared in amazement as Bobbi disappeared from sight. What was going on here?

Another piece to the puzzle, Ty thought as they started out riding alongside the buggy. Another piece of the puzzle that fit together in no way Ty could figure.

Silently they rode on across the valley. Champ kept his big blue roan near enough to Dahlia so that he could exchange an occasional word with the blond lady. Ty held back on the left flank, deep in thought, and the sullen Corby rode to the right.

The lady, Dahlia, was expertly competent, guiding the team of white horses down the steep, narrow trail to the flats below. The occasional patch of muddy water did nothing to slow her, nor did the rocks the storm had washed down from the cliffs at intervals. Ty watched her with admiration as she skillfully drove the team toward the mouth of the canyon.

Once out on the flats they turned westward. After a mile or so the land began to fold itself into low, sage-studded hills. Ty, surveying the land ahead and to either side as they rode, estimated that they were now within ten miles or so of Tucson, the area where the Shadow Riders had done most of their raiding.

Ty saw Studdard's hand rise, point and then lower again. Peering into the bright sunlight, he saw what the outlaw leader was indicating: two horsemen not far to the north riding in their direction. As they continued on their way, spread out as before, the strange horsemen angled nearer. Champ held up his mount and repositioned it on that side of Dahlia's buggy. Ty glanced at Corby, noting that the young deserter had slipped his Winchester from its scabbard and now rode with it across his saddle bow.

The approaching men continued to close the distance between themselves and the outlaw group. Now Ty was able to make out their features. One of them was long-jawed, unshaven. The other had a flowing black mustache and wore a white silk scarf around his neck. Why did they seem familiar to Ty . . . ?

Sperry and Michaels!

These were the two Arizona Rangers that Ty had encountered in Ethan Payne's office. Their job, Captain Payne had told Ty, was to attempt to locate the Shadow Riders' hideout. Now here they were, practically on top of it. If they recognized Ty, could they keep that recognition out of their eyes?

The two rangers slowly approached, slowly passed, their expressions unchanging. Sperry did touch his hat brim in the direction of Dahlia, but they barely glanced at the three men with her.

Ty released his breath in relief as the two walked their ponies on, their path leading them away from the entrance to the canyon trail. That had been close. Anything might have happened. And then it did.

From the corner of his eye, Ty saw Corby halt his horse, turn it, and lift his rifle to his shoulder.

Chapter Six

Ty heeled his sorrel roughly, sending it leaping toward Corby's dun pony. The two animals' shoulders collided, jarring both riders. Ty was ready for it, however; he had kicked free of his stirrups and now threw himself against Corby, coming up under his Winchester before he could fire it. They fell together in a heap beside the horses which danced away, tossing their heads angrily.

Wynn quickly got to his feet and he struggled to maintain a grip on his rifle. Ty was having none of it. He swung a hard right hook which bounced against Corby's skull just above the ear. Corby staggered a little, and Ty was able to take the Winchester by the barrel, twist it away from Wynn and toss it aside.

Enraged, Corby rushed at Ty, winging wild rights and lefts which Ty was able to duck or block. Ty jabbed a sharp left into Corby's face, bringing blood gushing from his nose. A second right buckled Corby's knees and he collapsed to the ground. Ty heard the approaching horse behind him and he spun to see Studdard on his big blue roan, the hammer of his Colt revolver eared back.

"Stop it," Champ said in a cold, quiet voice, "or I'll shoot the both of you. What's this about?"

"He jumped me," Corby said, wiping blood and dust from his face with the back of his hand. "Just when I had 'em in my sights!"

"Damn right I jumped you!" Ty said with heat. "Are you crazy, Corby? You were ready to start a shootout with Miss Dahlia in the middle of it? What would the boss think about that?"

"They could have been anybody!" Corby protested. He turned his head and spat more blood out. His eyes were wild as they met Ty's. "Could have been lawmen!"

"They could have been anybody," Ty agreed. "Maybe nothing but two saddletramps. But if you'd gone to shooting, they damn sure would have shot back and maybe hit Miss Dahlia!" Ty shook his head with disgust. "You plain have no sense, Corby."

"Champ, I . . ." Corby began, passionately pleading his case.

"The man's right, Corby," Champ said in a flat, cold voice. "It was a damn fool stunt. Get mounted. We've got places to go."

Champ swung his horse away from them, holstering his pistol. Dahlia, Ty noticed, only waited quietly in her buggy, showing no sign of being disturbed by the ruckus.

In her world, the world she had been brought up in, such clashes between men were such a common occurrence that they didn't even deserve notice.

The buggy started on. Studdard took up his position beside it. It was over. But not to Corby. His eyes reflected fierce bitterness, an anger that could not be stilled. Ty had done more than thwart him; he had belittled Corby in Studdard's eyes. Ty knew full well that this was the only thing Corby could not stand—to be regarded as a smaller man. Ty had already gathered up the reins to his sorrel. Now as he swung aboard he heard Corby mutter from behind him.

"I won't forget this, Ty. Once we might have been friends, but no more. I won't forget this if I live a hundred years."

The day continued clear and warm. The coolness of the storm had passed. The desert under the horses' hoofs was dry again, like it had never rained. The land began to rise steadily. The sun was nearly overhead when they came upon a narrow road made of crushed white quartz leading up to a low shelf of land where four or five live oaks and one sycamore tree flourished. The house the trees sheltered was low, of whitewashed adobe with red Spanish tiles on the roof.

The buggy turned that way and Dahlia's escort followed. Tall, whiplike ocotillo bushes were scattered across the land, their scarlet blooms providing the only color on the drab desert.

Two men with rifles appeared without warning in the road before them and Studdard held up a hand, halting Ty and Corby. As the buggy passed the riflemen, Champ held a brief meeting with them.

Once only, as the buggy negotiated a turn in the road, Ty caught a glimpse of Dahlia looking back. A brilliant smile parted her lips. A smile that seemed to be directed at him, and Ty wondered . . .

"Let's go, boys," Champ said, riding back to them. "Now we can put some ground under us."

Champ lifted his roan into a distance-devouring canter and they raced the sun westward. Once, through a notch in the low dark hills, Ty thought he spotted the city of Tucson, but they were angling away from it, and he could not be sure.

An hour later they were atop a rocky knoll studded with patches of nopal cactus. Champ sat his horse for a long minute, before swinging down and taking a pair of field glasses from his saddlebags. The outlaw seemed to be mentally mapping the terrain below, though what he was studying was a question.

From where he stood holding his jittery sorrel, Ty could see what appeared to be a ramshackle ranch made of four or five weather-beaten buildings that could have been abandoned. No horses. No cattle. What appeared to be a water tank stood near the largest of the buildings. A barbed-wire fence ran away into the far distances, shining in the sunlight. Champ continued to study the layout, carefully, slowly. Ty would have given a lot to use those field glasses himself for a few minutes. What was Champ looking at? What did the outlaws have planned?

"That'll work fine," Champ said to himself, still holding the binoculars to his eyes. "Just fine."

He put the field glasses away, swung aboard his horse and nodded to Ty and Corby. "Let's get home, men. I've seen all there is to see."

Corby began to sulk. He was obviously disappointed. Perhaps he had been looking forward to adventure, to gunplay. Ty was disappointed as well, but for different reasons. The Shadow Riders had something planned, obviously. Something that should be reported to the Rangers. But Ty had no idea what it was, nor any idea in the world how he could send word to Payne if he did know.

It was an experience in frustration. Champ was the only one who seemed relatively pleased. Sitting his silver-mounted saddle, he tugged his hat lower against the brilliance of the sun and led the way homeward across the broad desert.

The barracks and the stable were nearly empty when they reached the home ranch in the middle of the afternoon. Only the army bay horses remained in the corral. Champ had ridden off to report to the boss. Bill Cox was the only man around the barracks when Ty swung down from the sorrel. Corby had ridden his dun pony directly to the barn, still simmering.

"Hello, Ty," Bill said in greeting as Ty stepped up onto the porch.

"Bill," Ty answered. "You the only one home?"

"Me and George."

"Who?"

"George Hubler," Bill explained. "He's the man that rode in with me. You'll see him around. Easy enough to recognize. He's got a folded-over ear and only one of his eyes looks at you directly. He really wanted to be in the army, but the old troopers were always giving him hell."

Another one, Ty thought, glancing toward the barn where Corby had disappeared.

"Everybody else, or nearly everybody, rode out toward Titusville. They were saying there's a nice little bank there. I wanted to go, but I'm still the fresh meat." Bill smiled. "You know how that goes."

Ty nodded. Bill, it seemed, still had not learned about asking too many questions, about telling everything he knew.

"Bert rode with them, then?" Ty tried, but Bill's face was a blank.

"Don't know him, I guess," Bill said with an apologetic smile.

There was little in this whole puzzling situation that Ty found more frustrating than not knowing if Bert was here, who he was, and if he still had a method of getting information to the authorities.

A low, mournful sound caught both men's attention. Turning, they saw a young man dragging himself up onto the porch. He crawled toward Bill, his pitiful cries muffled with pain. Bill went to one knee and turned the man over.

His face was a mask of blood. There was a long, deep gash over one swollen eye.

"It's George," Bill told Ty. "George, what happened to you? Tell me!"

"Let's get him onto his bunk," Ty said, taking the young man's feet. A concerned Bill took the shoulders and they maneuvered George in through the barracks door and to his bunk.

"I'll get a cloth," Ty said. Bill squatted down beside George, trying to comfort the badly beaten man.

"Who would've done this?" Bill asked. "Who?"

Ty shook his head. With a damp towel he cleaned George's face and then pressed the cloth against the gash over his eye. "Someone'll have to sew that," Ty said. "You any good at stitching?"

"Who would have done such a thing?" Bill repeated instead of answering. "We should report this to someone . . ." He fell silent, knowing himself that things were not done that way here. Reporting it would only bring a laugh in response.

"I'll look for a needle and thread," Ty said. He himself had no doubt as to who had beaten George. How many men were on the ranch now anyway?

The cook had returned to the kitchen and was tying on his apron when Ty went in. "Have you got a needle and thread handy?" Ty asked the Mexican.

"For . . . ? What do you need for? Bridle?"

"To stitch up a man," Ty told him. "He got his eye busted open."

"Oh, yes?" the Mexican said. "I will take care of that. I am very good at stitching. I get a lot of practice here."

Together they returned to George's bedside where Bill waited anxiously, watching his friend. "He told me what happened," Bill said as the cook knelt to examine George's split eyebrow and thread his needle.

"What?" Ty asked.

"Tell him, George."

George winced as the cook took his first stitch; he kept his eyes closed tightly. "I was mucking out the barn like I was supposed to," George said. "Raking everything back toward the door to add to the pile outside. I didn't know anybody was there. I stepped on his foot . . ."

"Stepped on a man's foot and he got beaten like this!" Bill said angrily. Every trace of humor had vanished from the blond kid's normally cheerful face. "I'm going to take care of this!" Bill vowed, getting to his feet.

Ty put a restraining hand on his arm. "He'll shoot you," Ty warned.

"Who? You know who it was, then?"

"I have a good idea," Ty answered. "He likes shooting people. You don't even have a gun, Bill."

"You could loan me yours, Ty," Bill said fiercely.

Ty shook his head. "No, I won't. So far it's a beating—a bad beating, a mean beating—but only that. Let's not let it escalate to murder."

Bill shook his head angrily. His disappointment in Ty was obvious. It was then that they heard the scraping of boot leather across the barracks floor and, looking that way, they saw Corby enter, hat tilted back, a crooked smile on his lips.

"He all right?" Wynn asked. He stood three paces away, hand resting lazily on his gun butt.

"*You* did this?" Bill asked in a strangled voice. Ty again placed a restraining hand on Bill's arm.

"He mouthed off to me," Corby said with a shrug. "I wasn't going to take it from him."

"You're a damn liar!" Bill hissed.

Corby had turned away from them. Now he stopped and spun around to face Cox. "I don't take that either," Corby said. "Not from any man."

Corby's hand still rested on his Colt's handle, lightly caressing it.

Ty had had enough. "Back off, Corby. This time I mean it. First you beat someone up like this because he was clumsy. Then you take it into your head that you might want to shoot down an unarmed man. I'm neither, Corby," Ty said in a low voice as he shifted his feet slightly. "I'm not clumsy. And I'm carrying a gun. Make your play or shut up and get over it."

"You wouldn't . . ." Corby said, but there was some shakiness in his voice. He continued to glower at Ty, his hand hovering inches from his gun butt. Ty watched the changes in Corby's eyes. Much could be read there. Corby was not afraid of Ty, but unsure that he could take him in a gunfight. Ty, after all, was not Spud. Still other eyes were on him now, those of the cook, of Cox and the injured Huber. If he refused to draw, if he backed down, word of it would circulate around the camp. And men would brand him a coward! That was one thing Corby would find intolerable after having gone this far to build a reputation.

Ty saw all these thoughts flicker through Corby's eyes in fractions of a second. Then he saw Corby brace himself, setting his feet wider apart, and watched as the doubt in Corby's eyes hardened into hateful determination.

It might have been that Corby was going to draw then, but a voice called from the doorway. "Are you up to it again, Corby? Lower that gun hand and step away!"

Studdard's voice was unmistakably angry and there was an implicit threat in his words. Corby glanced at the outlaw chief and attempted an explanation. Champ cut him off. "You got Spud, Corby. Today you almost started something that might have put Miss Dahlia in the line of fire. Now you want to draw down on Cannfield with three unarmed men gathered around behind him." The lantern-jawed outlaw shook his head. "You want to fight, we'll find you plenty of fighting, but I won't have you thinning out *my* herd."

Champ removed his silver-banded hat and wiped back his graying dark hair. Frowning briefly, he made a decision.

"Get your gear together and go over to the other barracks, Corby. When he gets back, tell Jake Skaggs I sent you. Let him handle you."

Skaggs was the other field commander of the Shadow Riders. It was he who had ridden out to knock over the Titusville Bank. Ty had only seen the man once. Blocky and gruff, he seemed unlikely to put up with any shenanigans from Corby.

With Champ gone, Corby sullenly snatched up his few possessions and started toward the door with one hateful backward glance at Ty whom he undoubtedly blamed for his falling into disfavor with Studdard.

"You know, I think that was close," the Mexican said, rising from the work he had been doing on Huber's eye. "Champ, when he gets mad, he is very quick to draw his own gun, and I do not think he likes that Corby."

No, Ty reflected and he thought he knew why. Brawling, cussing, the occasional flare-up were to be expected. But even among the outlaw band, not so different from the regular army, some order had to be maintained. Some sort of discipline. Corby had shown himself, at least in Studdard's eyes, to be a loose cannon.

"I don't think we've heard the last of him," Cox said soberly.

"No," Ty agreed, "I don't think so either. Corby doesn't learn his lessons easily."

Huber asked weakly, "How do I look, Bill?" With his ear folded over, with his one bad eye that didn't seem to track right, a monstrous lump on his forehead and fresh stitches crosshatching his eyebrow, he looked like hell, Ty thought, but Cox smiled widely and ruffled George's dark hair.

"You'll do, George. Get some sleep now."

That was exactly what Ty felt like doing, but there was still a lot of daylight left and there was still a chance that he might be able to learn something useful.

Checking in with Tully, the wrangler, Ty made arrangements to borrow a fresh horse. His sorrel had had enough for one day, and the frisky young palomino Tully offered him needed exercise.

Tully gave Ty a lot of instructions on how to handle the half-broken young pony, but didn't question Ty's need for a horse. Tully's world, as Ty had observed earlier, began and ended with the horse herd.

Ty saddled and slipped the bit to the balky palomino. He had his own excuses made already. Should Storch happen to stop him and ask where he was going, he would tell him that they had asked him to return to the cattle herd and he was already late. If, on the other hand, he met the cattle herd and was challenged, he would simply say Storch sent him out. If there were any grumbling about him being a day late, he would just scratch his head, blame Storch and ride away.

The day remained mild. A few clouds, stretched thin by the prevailing north wind, drew pennants against the pale blue sky. The palomino settled in after a few miles and it was a pleasure to ride from then on. In passing, he glanced up at the dark form of the granite house standing high on the forbidden mesa, and he wondered again about Bobbi and her meeting with Dahlia.

Only once did the young horse Ty rode show any sign of skittishness and that was when they came upon a coyote slinking from the thicket with a jackrabbit in its jaws. By then Ty was farther east than he had ridden before. He passed two long-horned steers that glanced up from their browsing, giving him the evil eye, but he left them alone. An hour later he passed a small camp. Two men who were strangers to him were hunched near a low fire, boiling coffee. They were standing watch at the head of a narrow canyon with a wire fence on crooked posts strung loosely across it. Behind this, Ty saw a small herd of gathered cattle, mixed whiteface and longhorn.

Ty lifted a hand to the two and they waved back with only meager curiosity. Ty grinned. One advantage the code of secrecy in the valley offered was that no one knew where or why any other man was riding.

The dark eastern hills were nearer now. Low, mostly barren, they indicated that the far boundary of the outlaw range had been reached. Ty halted the palomino and mopped at his face with his bandana, wiping out the sweat band of his hat. The wind was cooler now, chilling the flesh beneath his damp shirt.

"What now?" he asked the palomino. The horse twitched one of its white ears and stamped its feet impatiently as if to reply that if the human on his back didn't know where he was going, he certainly didn't.

Ty started forward, moving northward, following the long arc of the hills. It was brushier here, with a lot of sumac, chia and sage crowded together. He saw no hoofprints marked in the winding path he traveled, but there was much cattle sign. About the time Ty had decided to give up on his expedition and return to the home ranch before darkness fell, he began hearing small, plaintive noises. Frowning, he halted the palomino again, and stood in the stirrups, looking around.

The sound continued, growing louder, and Ty recognized it for what it was, although he could see nothing at all through the brush. He started the palomino forward again.

Breaking through the screen of chaparral, he came upon the trapped calf.

How it had done it was anyone's guess, but the fearful, white-faced dogie had managed to slip off the trail into a narrow weather-cut gully beside it. It looked up miserably at Ty and tried to scramble out of the ditch as it must have many times before, but the walls of the gully were too steep and its legs too weak.

Ty uncoiled his lariat and walked to the edge of the cut. His second try settled the loop around the calf's neck and Ty went to the palomino, mounting it. He walked the horse slowly forward and glancing over his shoulder he watched as the stunned, wobbly calf reached flat ground to stand there bleating and trembling.

With a grin Ty retrieved his loop and swatted the calf on the flank. Startled, the animal walked forward, still bawling, following the trail that eventually led to the makeshift cattle corral where hopefully the calf's mother was waiting.

Ty had already fastened his coiled lariat onto the saddle before it slowly dawned on him. There was brush crowding the narrow flat where he stood, but much of it was broken and trampled. Many animals had come this way, not long ago. Leading the palomino through the brush, he discovered the tracks entering the valley seemed to go on forever.

He was standing at the head of a second trail leading out of the outlaw range.

Chapter Seven

Ty stood looking down the long mountain trail, the evening breeze shifting his palomino horse's mane and tail, and pressed his shirt to his back. He hoped to find the hidden trail, almost expecting to since logic dictated that there had to be another way in and out of the valley, a trail that could be used by cattle. The southern trail, winding, steep and narrow, obviously was unsuitable. Still Ty stood uncertainly, a sort of lingering disbelief in his mind. He caught himself dwelling on these thoughts, and mentally jolted himself awake.

Swinging onto his horse, he sat still and silent for several minutes, searching the long valley behind him. He saw no sign of man or animal; nothing moved but the brush ruffled by the afternoon breeze. Heeling the palomino, he started down the trail, needing to survey it. Were there also lookouts perched near this trail, their rifle sights ready to be fixed on any intruder? Although Ty had seen no horse tracks, he rode on with care. Fifty yards along he had a clear view of the length of the trail. Rather than winding its way up through the rocky canyon as the southern trail did, this one seemed to just slough off the hills after the first narrow pass was cleared. There was no place for snipers to conceal themselves beside the trail as it widened and spread itself into a sort of fan falling toward the long desert flats below.

Studying the trail, Ty felt a vast relief. And, despite himself, he also felt a moment's urge to just continue on down it, to ride away from the high valley and all of its troubles. Ty rode on only a little farther, trying to get his bearings. Where did the trail ultimately find its end? Was there a hidden outpost down there, some small pueblo hidden in the afternoon mist? It was impossible to tell. He had accomplished all that he could hope to accomplish today, and he turned the palomino and guided it back through the brush until he was once again on the valley flats.

With no reason to ride slowly, with nothing more to discover, he nudged the horse's flanks with his heels and hung on as the young, eager pony broke into a ground-devouring run.

When Ty reached the home ranch, the sun was heeling over toward the western horizon, the sky near the far hills a cobalt blue. There was no color in the sky, but it would be painted there soon. Reaching the corral, he swung down under the watchful eye of Tully who wanted to be certain that his young charge had not been ridden too hard. Stroking the palomino's sleek neck, Tully nodded with approval.

Ty stripped off his saddle and slipped the bit. Tully watched, then reached for his curry comb. Ty asked him, "Dinner ready yet?"

"Don't know," Tully said, his eyes on his work. "You'd better forget dinner though, and saddle up. You'll be late and Champ don't like people who are late."

Champ? Did that mean that the outlaws were riding out again? Ty was stiff and saddle sore. He had ridden more miles already than he could count. Frowning, he studied Tully's face, hoping to catch some indication that the wrangler was pulling his leg. He wasn't.

From the barn someone called out Ty's name, and shouldering his saddle, carrying his blanket and bridle in his free hand, he started that way to find Bill, his cheerful face showing anxiety.

"Glad you're back!" Bill said, putting his hand on Ty's shoulder as they walked into the barn. "They were calling your name a while back, but nobody knew where you were."

Ty nodded and trudged the length of the barn heavily, going to the stall where his sorrel, fed, watered and rested, waited for him.

"You know everything, Bill. Where are we riding?"

"Ty," Bill grinned, "I didn't ask. "I'll get your pony ready for you. Maybe that'll give you a minute to grab a few biscuits from the kitchen."

"I appreciate it," Ty answered. "How's George doing?"

"He was up and working this afternoon," Bill said as he smoothed the saddle blanket on the sorrel's back. "Says he's got one hell of a headache, though."

Ty crossed the yard to the back kitchen door and slipped inside. Storch glanced up at him edgily. "You missed dinner. Where in hell have you been?"

"You told me to ride over to the cattle herd," Ty said easily, snatching up two thick slices of the cook's yeasty bread and slapping a slab of ham between them.

"That was *yesterday*, Cannfield!"

"Yes, it was," Ty said around a bite of the sandwich. "And yesterday they told me that they wanted me back out there today. What am I supposed to do? Who's boss around here, anyway?"

"Right now it's Champ Studdard," Storch said, frowning. "I'd get myself ready to ride if I was you."

"I'm all ready," Ty said as he saw Bill Cox leading his saddled sorrel pony into the front yard where half a dozen men already sat their horses, waiting for Champ. "See you, Storch."

"Cuttin' it close," he heard Storch mutter and then Ty was in the yard, swinging onto the sorrel moments before Studdard appeared through the oak trees, riding in from the big house. Ty thought he could see the boss himself standing at one of the front windows, watching his army assemble, but the distance was too great and the house too dark to be sure.

Studdard had a little speech to make. "Some of the new men here might not have gotten the word. Some of the old-timers might need reminding. There's a reason we leave on the dot for our night rides. We need to be in the canyon while there's still light to ride by. You all know that trail—nobody wants to navigate it in darkness.

"On the other hand we want the cover of darkness when we're ready to go out onto the desert flats. We have this timed carefully so that we have time to gather at the foot of the trail and rest our mounts for a few minutes before last light is gone."

Champ finished up. "So when you're told it's a night ride, you be ready, guns oiled, saddles cinched, set to ride when I arrive. Anyone who dawdles or fails to show faces my severe displeasure."

Ty thought that Champ's eyes flickered toward him, but it was too brief a look to be sure. The warning seemed to be a general remark, but one to be kept in mind. He didn't want to know what facing Champ's "severe displeasure" entailed.

They rode in a loose column as the western sky took on the color of flowering purple sage. A few of the veteran outlaws spoke in low voices, and once a man laughed out loud, but for the most part they were silent as the armed body made its way through the lengthening shadows.

By the time they had made their way down the canyon trail and gathered at its foot, the covering shadows were nearly complete. Only a last, thin crimson pennant hung in the western sky to mark the passing of the sun. If anyone but Champ knew their destination, it was not mentioned. Ty thought this another flaw in the code of secrecy they labored under. Men prepared for a job were more likely to perform it well.

At a signal unapparent to Ty in the darkness, the riders moved out into the desert. The moon was late-rising these nights and they would have hours before its illumination could give them away. There was only the creaking of saddle leather, the chink of bridle chains, the plodding of the horses' hoofs to break the silence. The stars had begun to blink on, and here and there Ty could pick out the white markings on a horse's face, and the glint of starlight on the metal of the guns they wore.

For the rest it was darkness and silence as Ty rode along with the outlaw gang, inexorably carried by the tide of horsemen toward some unknown battlefield. He wondered again what he was doing among them. How had he let Ethan talk him into this? It didn't matter, he supposed. He had nothing to live for since Kathleen's death. Everyone's got to die sometime; at least he would be dying for a cause.

They crested a low, humped hill where the scent of sage was heavy and Champ halted his troupe. He summoned a man Ty knew only by the name Dink. Dink was a sloppily put-together man who seemed to be pure flab. His chin sagged into his throat; his small eyes even seemed to droop. He was reputed to be a stone killer.

After meeting with Champ, Dink rode back along the column, selecting four men with his stubby pointing finger. Ty was chosen for Dink's part in whatever was to come, and the five riders separated from Champ's outlaw soldiers. Dink's instruction were clear and terse.

"Mind you don't call out anybody's name for them to hear. You see a man with a star, shoot to kill."

Reaching the skyline of the hills, Ty could only now make out their target for that night. It bore no resemblance to the rough settlement that Champ had scouted earlier in the day, and was in fact miles to the south. Below he could see a stage station, made evident by the coach standing before the low adobe building, its traces on the ground, horses penned up for the night. There was a pole corral beside this building where the horses dozed, and another adobe building beyond. This was a freight office, Ty knew instantly. Three high-wheeled wagons stood in a row behind the windowless building; a light glowed dully in a single window.

This was the Shadow Riders' target. Freight was only conveyed in one manner across all of the Southwest—by wagon. Everything from a lady's looking glass to barstools, food stuffs and finery was carried on the big wagons. They, too, had to stop to rest the horses, to change teams or transfer goods to another route. This was one such stopping-off place.

Dink held up his group of raiders, tying his bandana over his face as a mask. The others followed suit. Dink's muffled voice instructed, "We're going to spread out along the back of the freight depot. Don't let anybody cross from the stage stop. It's likely that the teamsters and line police will be holed up over there for supper, drinks and gossip.

"You can bet they'll come at a run when Champ blows the front door off the depot."

Carefully they wound their way down the slope of the hill, spreading out as they reached the flat where the two adobe block buildings stood side by side. Smoke curled lazily from the stage station to haze the stars. Ty found himself nearest to the stage stop as they unsheathed their long guns and took up positions.

The opposition was to be freight line operatives, men who rode shotgun on the massive wagons, not regular law officers. From what Ty knew of this breed, however, they were as tough and sure-handed as any sworn officer. They had to be, guarding goods across miles of Indian country, past bands of outlaws who waited to strip them of whatever they were carrying.

Their freight often included gold and silver money, bonds and notes for the small far-flung Western banks. These would be Champ's objective.

Ty dismounted although the two other men he could see in the darkness remained in the saddle. Minutes passed slowly as he watched from one knee, wondering what he could possibly do to avert murder without giving himself away. Nothing, he decided unhappily . . . The movement at the south end of the small clump of buildings caught his eye, and he saw the shadowy band of mounted men enter the village, spreading out as they went. The stage stop and freight depot were now completely surrounded.

Ty was caught off guard when the raid began. Champ had wasted no time setting an explosive charge against the front door of the freight office and touching it off. The explosion flung debris into the sky, forming small dusty comets. Three shots were fired from inside the freight office and then none as the raiders stormed the building. From the stage stop a knot of armed men streamed into the night like angry hornets and the gun battle began as the waiting Shadow Riders opened fire on the freight line's operatives. Ty saw one man fall face-first to the rough ground, then saw three others withdraw, guns blazing into the confines of the stage stop.

Someone had slipped out a window or an unseen door and circled to the rear of the building. Now two shots from the rifleman whipped past Ty's head. He ducked low, holding his own fire, unwilling to shoot down an innocent man.

Dink had no such qualms. He levered four closely spaced .44 slugs through the barrel of his Winchester and ducked down behind his shying horse as the man below slipped into the paddock and hid himself behind a panicked group of stage ponies, before he fired twice more in return. Dink shouted out above the general tumult. "Your man, Cannfield, get him!" the outlaw chief bellowed, forgetting his own order not to use names.

Ty was left with few choices. To fail to obey Dink would lead to his banishment or severe punishment; he did not know which. To shoot down the man guarding the stage stop was pure murder. Dropping the reins to his sorrel, Ty started down the dark hillside on foot. Dink yelled something else he could not hear above the constant roar of the guns. Champ, he saw now, was quickly emptying the freight office of its portable valuables.

Slipping, sliding, Ty made his way to the flats as another bullet from the unseen rifleman dusted the earth near his feet. Twelve more long strides took Ty to the corral. He went to the ground and rolled under, the hoofs of the milling herd passing too close for comfort, more dangerous than a stray bullet.

The rifleman held his fire. Either he could not see Ty or he was afraid of hitting the horses. Whichever, it gave Ty time to creep through the shadows at the border of the pen and come up behind the stage station itself. He stood there, back against the adobe wall, chest rising and falling heavily. Near at hand the rifle roared again. Ty saw the stab of flame as the rifleman, having shifted his aim, loosed a shot at Dink's men along the hillside.

The shooter had taken shelter behind a crate just inside the pole corral. Ty could make out the barrel of his Winchester, see a shock of hair above the edge of the crate. Ty rushed him.

He took four running steps and rolled across the crate, landing on top of the startled rifleman. Ty drove his right fist into the man's face, sending him staggering back and to the ground. Ty stood on his wrist and wrenched the rifle away, hurling it across the corral posts into the brush beyond.

The man's eyes glittered angrily in the starlight as he stared up at Ty hovering over him.

Ty whispered savagely, "I'm going to fire my pistol. Twice. After that you remain still and don't make a peep or I'll be forced to kill you."

The man could only stare uncertainly at Ty who thumbed back the hammer of his Colt and fired twice into the ground, inches from the rifleman's head. Then, with a meaningful glance, he sprinted across the corral, pushing the horses out of his path and dashed back to the hillside. The shooting below was tapering off now. Already some of the Shadow Riders, their saddlebags loaded with booty, were withdrawing into the desert. Dink had moved over to

Cannfield's position. The fat man whispered, "Did you get him?"

"That's what you sent me to do, isn't it?" Ty growled in response.

Dink nodded admiringly. "Mount up and be ready to ride the moment you see Champ hit the end of the street."

In less than half a minute Ty heard the sound of pounding hoofbeats and he saw Champ, readily identifiable with that silver-mounted saddle, riding low across the withers, heeling his blue roan toward the outskirts of town. A fusillade of gunfire from the stage station followed him and his companions.

"Now!" Dink said. "Hit the trail running!"

Ty obeyed instantly. From below, now that the body of outlaws had cleared the town, half a dozen men had appeared to take potshots at the rear guard of the Shadow Riders. Ty flagged the sorrel with his hat, riding hell for it up the brushy hill and over the crown to safety as bullets flew wildly around them. A quarter of a mile on, Ty halted the weary sorrel beside Dink and asked, "Did we lose anybody?"

"Just Quarters with us. I saw two men down in the street from Champ's bunch." Then Dink, looking anxious, said, "We'd better keep moving. Never know—a few of them wagon toughs might feel mad enough to gather up their ponies and come after us."

Ten minutes later they came upon Champ lying against the rough earth, shot to pieces.

Ty leaped down from his sorrel's back before the horse had stopped. Champ was lying sprawled against the ground, his blue roan standing nervously over him. The silver-banded hat lay crumpled near at hand. Ty crouched down beside the outlaw leader as Dink swung heavily from his horse and lumbered up to join them.

"Where'd they get you?" Ty asked.

Champ tried a smile but he couldn't hold it through the pain. "Where didn't they get me?"

"You'll make it," Ty said.

"Damn right I'll make it!" Champ said angrily. "I'll make it just to go back to teach those wagon hounds a lesson. Next time I'll set fire to the place and when they come running out, I'll shoot them down like rats." The last half of this dark vow was muffled by an uncontrollable groan of pain.

"We'll get you back, Champ," Dink promised.

"I can't make it that far," Champ told the fat man. "I'm bleeding bad. Besides that, Dink, I need you to catch up with the boys. If they don't see me around . . . there's a couple of them, Beech among them, that I never trusted. Now him and his cronies have their saddlebags full of gold, and if no one's there to watch them, they just may take a notion to cut and run." Champ coughed again, reached out and gripped Dink's shirt sleeve. "You catch up, Dink. Keep an eye on them for me."

"What about you, Champ?" Dink asked with more concern than Ty would have expected from the fat killer.

"I'll be all right. Cannfield will take me. He knows the way."

"What way?" Ty asked in confusion.

"I can't make it to the valley, but I think I can hang on as far as Dahlia's place. You remember how to find it, Cannfield."

"I do," Ty answered.

"That's what we'll do then," Champ said, coughing up a bit of blood. "Get me onto my pony. If you see me start to sway, Cannfield, tie my boots to the stirrups to keep me aboard. But get me to Dahlia's."

Chapter Eight

The two horses plodded heavily up the crushed quartz trail leading to Dahlia's red-roofed adobe house. The ocotillo bushes, twenty feet high or more, cut stark, thorny silhouettes against the starry sky. Champ's moans of pain had ceased a few miles back. After the first mile he had slumped in his saddle and then fallen to the earth. Ty tied his legs to his stirrups and continued on, as instructed. He couldn't even be sure if the outlaw leader was dead or alive as he rode sprawled across the blue roan's withers.

Not unexpectedly two armed guards appeared on the trail leading to Dahlia's house. Ty heard the lever of a Winchester being worked and a hoarse voice spoke challengingly. "If you got business here, better tell us what is it."

"My name's Cannfield. I've got Champ Studdard here. He's shot up pretty bad."

Without realizing it, he fell off to sleep as the murmuring continued and they worked steadily on, trying to patch Champ back together. He awoke with a start to find Dahlia leaning over him. There was a smile on her lips. She still wore her wrapper. Her hair had been gathered back now, tied at the nape of her neck with a pale blue ribbon.

Ty sat up abruptly. He looked past her at the sofa where Champ had lain. He was still there—he was alive.

"He going to make it?" Ty asked, stifling a yawn.

"I think so," Dahlia said. "If he lasts until morning, his chances are good. You," she instructed, "get up and follow me. You need a real bed."

Doing as he was commanded, Ty followed Dahlia down another corridor and into a bedroom decorated very femininely. The canopied bed was covered with a frilly pink spread. There were matching pillows arranged at the head of the bed. Secret, faintly alluring fragrances filled the air. It was altogether the sort of room a man did not feel comfortable in.

Dahlia noticed his unease, smiled and began removing the pillows and bedspread. "The mattress is a good one. Better than you've had lately, I'd wager."

She kept on chattering as she folded the spread, tossed the pillows onto a nearby chair and folded the blankets back. Ty did not hear half of what she said. His attention had been drawn to a large picture in a silver frame standing on the dressing table. He picked it up to look at it more closely. He could feel Dahlia at his side.

"You and Bobbi," he said, not looking away from the

picture. Dahlia appeared much the same in the picture, but a little younger. Bobbi wore a flouncy dress. Her dark hair was much longer, curling over her slender shoulders.

"That's us!" Dahlia agreed with a note of pleasure. She did not seem surprised that Ty knew Bobbi. He glanced at her curiously. "Oh, I know you've met my sister. She and I had a private talk this morning—surely you saw her up at the valley house."

"Yes." But what had Bobbi been doing there? Ty thought he had figured out Dahlia's role in matters, but he could be wrong about that as well. Bobbi and her sister probably had an arrangement to visit each other when Dahlia was going to be in the valley—nothing mysterious about that. But why would Bobbi ever agree to cross the threshold of a man she so obviously hated? He wanted to ask questions, but he wasn't sure that he even knew the right ones to ask.

Dahlia cut through his musings. "Get to bed now. We all need some sleep after a night like this."

Without another word she turned down the lantern wick and with a last, brief smile, swept out of the room, leaving Ty to crawl gratefully into the soft bed and sleep as the late-rising silver moon coldly illuminated the unfamiliar room.

Only Eric was around when Ty rose late in the morning and emerged, sleepy-eyed from the room. Passing the parlor, he saw Champ looking extremely pale, but sleeping peacefully. Eric stood in the center of the room like a man standing guard.

"How is he?" Ty asked.

"Looks like he'll make it," Eric answered as if it were none of Ty's business. "Your horse is out front, saddled and ready to ride. Soon as I heard you stirring, I had it brought around. Take this with you—it's from Miss Dahlia to the boss," he added, handing Ty a manila envelope with a red wax seal. If this wasn't a suggestion to depart, it sure sounded like one. Ty nodded to the mustached man and went out onto the porch into the heated glare of the desert morning. Still stiff and sore, he swung aboard the sorrel which seemed no more anxious to be moving on again than was Ty. No matter—when the man of the house suggests that you leave, a wise guest goes.

Ty saw no sign of the guards along the crushed quartz road. In fact he saw not another living thing throughout the morning as he and the sorrel pony labored their way home to the big valley. The air was cooler at that altitude, although the sun had ridden higher in the crystal blue sky.

The outlaw ranch was slumbering in inactivity when Ty rode to the barracks and wearily swung down. As his boots touched ground, a crowd began to gather. Bill Cox was there first, stretching out a hand.

"I'll see to your horse, Ty," the blond kid offered. Ty noticed Bill now wore a pistol on his hip.

The door to the barracks stood open and Storch waited there surrounded by a knot of outlaws, Dink prominent among them.

"How's Champ?" Dink asked.

"All right for now."

"I didn't think you'd even make it to Dahlia's, the way he was shot up," the flabby gunman said. He grinned and thumbed back his hat. "Good going, Cannfield."

A few other men offered their congratulations. Hands slapped him on the back as he entered the barracks. Storch was busy shooing them away.

"Give the man a break, fellows! He's had a long ride and must be hungry."

That was true enough, and Ty followed Storch into the kitchen where the smiling cook served a cup of coffee before he had even settled on the plank bench. A few of the raiders still hovered near the doorway. Gossip, tales of the trail were the only sort of entertainment to be had here, and they were eager to hear more of the details of Ty's ride.

Storch finally closed the door and told the Mexican cook, "Rustle up something special for Cannfield." Ty settled in gratefully to wait. There was nothing like being the hero of the moment, even if it was only for the moment—until the next act of reckless bravery by another man eclipsed the old time-worn story.

Ty had only taken the first sip of coffee before the outer door opened and an outlaw entered uncertainly. "The boss wants to see you, Cannfield," the messenger said.

Ty nodded, checked to make sure he still had the letter Dahlia had sent and went out into the brilliant day, leaving the promising scent of a thick steak frying in the pan behind him. Walking through the mottled shade of the tall oak trees, Ty approached the big house. A Winchester-equipped guard watched Ty's approach from the shadow of his hat brim, and he said, "Go on in. You're expected."

Ty removed his hat and walked the length of the hall. He started to rap on the frame of the open doorway, but the boss heard him coming.

"Come in, Cannfield," said the familiar, toneless voice and Ty entered to find the boss, his scarred face set in concentration, looking out across the empty land through the parted scarlet drapes. He turned, glanced at Ty and walked behind his wide desk where he settled himself. "Take a seat," he told Ty with a loose gesture of his hand.

Ty nodded and twisted a chair around to face the desk. Before he seated himself he fished the envelope from his pocket and placed it on the desk. The man with the scar eyed it for a long moment before picking it up, opening it with a silver letter knife and extracting the note. Ty could detect a womanly scent accompanying the letter even across the desk. The letter, slowly read, was placed aside as the boss lifted those snake eyes of his to Ty's.

"It seems that you have acquitted yourself well, Cannfield."

"Just did what I was told to do," Ty said carelessly.

"That is what I mean. A good soldier takes orders and follows them through. Miss Dahlia speaks well of you," he added, tapping the letter. "It seems agreed that you saved Champ's life. I value Champ highly, Cannfield. He, too, spoke well of you in his last report to me. He told me that you kept Miss Dahlia out of harm's way on the trail the other day." Quietly, intensely he added, "I value Miss Dahlia highly as well, Cannfield."

Ty said nothing. The man with the dreadful scar was thoughtful, silent for a long minute. Leaning forward, he clasped his hands together and told Ty, "Dink tells me that you showed a lot of courage last night. He says they were pinned down by a sniper and you rushed the rifleman on foot, took him out."

"There didn't seem to be any other way."

"I see. Cannfield, as you well know, Champ is out of action. I will miss him—he's a decisive commander. I have no choice but to move Dink up to replace him."

"Dink's brave—and he's loyal," Ty commented. Neither of them mentioned the reason that Ty had been dispatched to take Champ to Dahlia's house, beyond knowing the way. There had been the suspicion that some of the outlaws, tempted by the gold in their saddlebags, might just decide the time had come to cut their ties with the outfit, and Dink meant to keep an eye on them. This thought might have been revolving in the boss' mind as he nodded positively at Ty's use of the word "loyal" to describe Dink. Both knew that with Champ down, Dink himself could have been party to such a plan if he'd had the inclination.

"Glad to hear your assessment, Cannfield. It leads me to think that you, too, are a loyal man. Loyal to Dink, to Champ." He cleared his throat gently. "Dink is moving up into Champ's place as commander, Cannfield. You are going to take Dink's place as his lieutenant."

Ty frowned. "It may be that Dink would prefer a more seasoned man."

"I've already spoken to Dink. It was his suggestion, Cannfield. You're his right hand now. It's settled."

"Thank you, sir," Ty said, "I'll see that you . . ."

A voice from the open doorway interrupted Ty.

"Mingo! We've got a problem. You'd better come . . ."

If Ty had thought previously that the boss' eyes resembled those of a rattler, what he saw in them now was the look of one with fangs bared, ready to strike. The guard, the man who had greeted Ty on the porch, seemed to shrivel up in his skin, realizing instantly what he had done.

He had spoken the name of the man with no name.

Mingo.

"We're through, Cannfield," the man with the scar said in a voice that was controlled now, but ready to explode. "Talk to Dink."

Ty nodded, rose and squeezed past the panicked guard. The heavy door to the office was banged shut behind Ty as he made his way down the corridor.

Mingo? The name was obviously only a nickname, and it meant nothing to Ty. But it could be very important to Ethan . . . if Ty could ever figure out how to get word of the outlaws' activities to the Ranger.

Ty's boots kicked up tiny puffs of dust as he crossed the yard, the recent rain just a memory. Passing the first barracks, that occupied by Jake Skaggs' soldiers, he saw a familiar face watching him from the porch. Word traveled fast in this camp, it seemed. Corby's eyes were filled with loathing and jealously.

Dink must have done some talking, for the look Corby gave Ty was one of a man betrayed, It was *Corby* who had proven himself, the look said. Corby who had been ready to fight out on the desert only to be humiliated in front of

Champ Studdard. Now Ty had risen to the rank of lieutenant while Corby's star was plummeting. Everyone knew there was a disgrace in his being transferred to Skaggs' band. Champ would not have shipped Corby off if he had been pleased with him.

Ty briefly considered pausing to talk to Wynn, but immediately jettisoned the idea. There was nothing further to be said between the two men.

Ty's steak was still in the frying pan when he reentered the kitchen. Cold, drier, greasier, he speared it out of the pan, tossed it onto a plate, cut himself a thick slice of bread and sat down to eat. The steak was still the best meal he had eaten for days. Thinking about it, Ty decided there wasn't a lot to be said for the outlaw way of life.

The day was still bright, the sun still hours away from sagging below the horizon. Ty tried resting on his bunk for a while, but everyone wanted to hear about the raid on the freight station, Champ's fate or that Ty was now second in command to Dink. After answering every question for the second time, Ty took his hat from the bedpost and went out, yawning, into the light of day. He didn't feel much like riding, but then he didn't have to stay in the saddle all afternoon, and a brief ride would get him away from the camp, perhaps give him time to think.

Tully, without animation, saw that Ty was provided with a fresh horse, a slightly bowlegged gray with an even temper and plenty of bottom. Hubler volunteered to saddle the horse for him despite Ty's objections.

"I owe it to you, Ty," George said. His eye was a swollen purplish ball, and he still moved stiffly. George also had been given a handgun, evidence of his new status. Ty shrugged and let him see to the gray. Smiling inwardly, Ty reflected that through no real intent, he had acquired a sort of celebrity in the outlaw camp. Well, he decided, it beat the alternative. He now had acceptance, trust and the ear of Dink if not of the boss—Mingo—himself.

Riding at an easy pace, Ty wracked his brain, trying to remember ever hearing of a man named Mingo, but he came up with nothing. He sifted through what he actually knew of the outlaw leader. It was very little.

From his speech Ty had pegged him as being from one of the border states, maybe Tennessee or Kentucky. Not from the Deep South, definitely, but neither did he have a Texas twang nor an Arkansas drawl. He was from somewhere south of the Mason-Dixon line. Ty felt sure of that, though it didn't do much to identify the man.

The nickname "Mingo" might have some meaning, but Ty could make nothing out of that. The military-like atmosphere of the outlaw camp, down to the barracks construction, and the occasional use of military designations—"field commander" or "lieutenant"—seemed to mark him for a former soldier, but that could mean nothing.

Ty guided the gray down into a narrow, sandy gully and up the far side. He realized that without any plan, he was riding southward, toward the big thicket and the mesa beyond. He glanced up to see the dark shadows of the stone house on the bluff high above him.

He shook himself mentally, trying to concentrate on the questions at hand and not the stone house and its occupants. *Mingo.* Why did the man never show himself unless absolutely necessary? He remained under self-imposed house arrest, secluded in his big house. Or did he? Mingo was a man of some sophistication; he had new tailor-made clothes. At times he must visit Dahlia. Maybe Mingo was not always home alone. He might even have a second life . . . in Tucson?

In Tucson he could have his clothes made, could listen to the local talk about gold shipments and army movements. What if he was a well-known citizen in Tucson, not known as Mingo but by some other name? A well-respected man with an excuse for long absences from the town. That was something to consider. It might be only a wild notion, but Ty meant to attempt to keep a closer watch on the big house from now on, to determine if Mingo was indeed moving about more than he had considered.

"Coming to call, are you?" the voice from the thicket said quietly and Ty, lost in thought, was brought sharply out of his daydreaming. He reached for his Colt and leaned low over the shoulder of the gray as he drew it. Laughter rang in his ears.

"I never took you for the nervous type," Bobbi said lightly as she approached him, riding the little paint pony Ty had seen her use the day before. Sheepishly, Ty holstered his pistol.

"What are you doing out here?" he asked, kneeing his horse up beside hers.

"Riding. If I stayed cooped up with Judd and Uncle Morgan, I'd go insane."

"Your uncle doesn't mind?"

"He doesn't like it, but what can he do? Tie me down?"

Bobbi asked brightly. She wiped a strand of her short dark hair from her eyes and smiled. She wore a white blouse, loosely fit, and black jeans. Ty tried to picture her in a flouncy dress with her hair long and curled.

"What are you thinking of?" Bobbi asked, frowning.

"In general, or now?"

"Just now."

"I was remembering how you looked in that picture I saw in Dahlia's house—the two of you all dressed up, smiling like it was a bright new day you wanted to remember."

"You were there?" Bobbi asked with ill-concealed surprise. "In *my* room!"

"That was your room? I had no idea," Ty answered as they started their horses forward. But he had known it, on some deep level. Yes, he admitted to himself, he had known that Bobbi had been there. He could feel her presence.

"How did you like it?" Bobbi asked.

"The room? I could do without the lacy stuff," Ty answered and Bobbi laughed again.

"I meant how did you like my sister's house?"

Ty thought. "Close," he replied. "Too close. Men guarding the trail, watching the house . . . It doesn't seem that Dahlia has much more freedom than you do."

"We're all prisoners in some way," Bobbi responded philosophically. After awhile she asked Ty, "How about you—don't you feel like a prisoner sometimes?"

Ty didn't answer. Yes, he did. But he had constructed much of his cell by himself.

They continued on without speaking for a while. The sun

was warm, the breeze fresh but not cool. The land seemed unpopulated. The sky itself was empty except for one high-soaring golden eagle. Ty was content to ride alongside the woman in silence.

"I wouldn't want to be an outlaw," Bobbi said at length. They had neared a lone oak standing on a low knoll, and Ty suggested they swing down. His own legs had had too much riding these past few days. He was still sore as they dismounted. He was silent, taking a long time to respond to her comment. They were settled on the ground, backs against the massive old oak tree before he answered.

"It wouldn't be my first choice as a way of life." He plucked at the dry grass beside his leg. The horses were tugging at the rough forage. Bobbi sat beside him, seemingly at peace, her wide brown eyes looking toward the distance as the breeze continued to play with her short dark hair.

"No friends, no future, no freedom," Bobbi said.

"A bit like your life, isn't it?" Ty said without thinking. Bobbi frowned. "Sorry," he apologized.

"It's all right."

"Why are you staying here, then?" Ty asked. "You could ride off, couldn't you? Maybe stay with your sister."

"That would never work. She has her own prison, as you've noted. Besides, I can't leave, won't leave until I've gotten back everything that is mine. Everything that my father built for us."

"Tell me," Ty encouraged.

Bobbi's mouth tightened. The light had faded from her eyes. She continued to look straight ahead. Sighing, she began. "My father discovered this valley. No white man had ever been here before. He scraped and worked and began bringing cattle up here. Built the stone house with his own two hands. Dahlia and I were still quite young. Our mother had died when I was three years old. Father doted on us. He nearly worked himself to death to provide, to build a legacy for us. Then they started to come."

"The outlaws?"

"We didn't know that was what they were at first. Father even welcomed Mr. Volker when he first arrived, told him to feel free to cut out a beef or two from our herd if they got needy. But they kept coming, and coming!" Bobbi said, her eyes now damp. "Ragged men, many of them wearing army uniforms. Deserters, scum, saddle tramps and hardened outlaws."

"Volker?"

"Yes. Him!" she said, inclining her head toward the outlaw camp. "Volker."

Ty frowned. Now the man with no name had two.

"When Father had enough he told Volker that he had abused his hospitality and ordered him out of the valley. Volker just laughed. He would stay as long as he wanted, he boasted. He would use the cattle as his own. None of us would be allowed to leave the valley."

"What happened?"

"We had ten cowhands by then, rough men, but mostly good ones. They weren't enough to fight off fifty outlaws. Men were killed as they rode herd, shot from ambush. Father was murdered. Dahlia and I were left alone with Judd and my Uncle Morgan who had arrived by then—Morgan was my mother's brother. Judd, his stepson."

"They didn't wish to fight, I take it."

"You mean because they are still alive?" Bobbi asked ruefully. "Truthfully, there wasn't much that Morgan could have done, but no, he did not wish to fight Volker and his men any longer. They cut a deal."

"Meaning, Volker got everything he wanted."

"Everything. Dahlia included. She was part of the price for peace."

"And you?" Ty asked.

"Me?" Bobbi laughed. "I was small, ornery and stubborn. I cut off my hair and turned myself into the worst sort of tomboy you'd ever hope to see . . ." She hesitated. "Besides, Dahlia would have none of it. She told Volker that she would go with him, but if I was ever touched, she'd cut his throat as he slept. Don't doubt it. You've never seen Dahlia when she's mad. I was left alone after that."

It was still a horrible story. What it would have been like to live through those years, growing up a young girl in this wilderness under those conditions, was beyond knowing.

"You said that you intend to get your land back," Ty said. "Any plan on how to do that?"

Bobbi laughed and shook her head. "I used to wait for my white knight to appear, but he never did come," she said.

"I understand that they're like that," Ty said. "Unreliable as hell."

Bobbi laughed again and shook her head. "So it seems." She looked directly at him and asked, "They call you Ty. Is that your real name?"

"Real enough. My mother named me Tyrone. My sisters, the other kids decided that was too long a name for me and it's been mostly Ty ever since. How about you? You can't have been christened Bobbi."

"No—Roberta, actually. I've almost always been called Bobbi, though. They say it suits me."

"It does," Ty agreed. "Roberta," he repeated thoughtfully. "Tell me, Bobbi—has anyone ever called you *Bert*?"

Chapter Nine

The blood seemed to drain out of Bobbi. Her eyes went wide with astonishment and then narrowed to suspicion. She got to her feet, dusting her jeans off. She looked away from Ty, eyes fixed on the far horizon.

"I don't know what you mean. Of course not," she said rapidly.

Ty stood and turned her by the shoulders to face him. Looking down into her brown eyes, he said, "I guessed right, didn't I?"

She looked down at her boot toes, at his face and then down again before she murmured, "How did you guess? How could you know?"

"Obvious, isn't it?" Ty asked, lifting her chin with one finger so that he could look again into her eyes, and smiled. "You're not what you seem to be. Neither am I."

"You're not Ty Cannfield, the outlaw?" Bobbi asked with uncertain hope.

"I'm Ty Cannfield. Not an outlaw. You have to trust me, Bobbi. I'm with the Arizona Rangers—I wouldn't tell you that if I didn't trust you."

"You sure fooled me!"

"I hope I've fooled everyone else as well. It wouldn't work any other way, would it?" Bobbi was silent for a long while, just studying his eyes. In embarrassment she said, "I liked you anyway, Ty . . . This makes it a lot easier to do so."

"I'm glad." There was a moment then when he felt like kissing her, but he did not. It would have been too much. She liked him, had said so—that was enough. There were things he needed to know, however.

"How have you managed it, Bobbi? Getting word out about impending outlaw raids?"

"You don't know?" she replied. "You've seen my messenger."

"You can't mean Dahlia!"

"Can't I? I do."

"But she's . . ."

"Volker's woman? No, she never has been. She's only with him by threat of force." Bobbi went on earnestly. "She's wanted to run for a long while, but then what would become of my uncle Morgan, Judd and me? There's no telling what Volker will do in one of his rages. She's playing a very dangerous game, Ty. We can only get information out after one of their visits, when Volker is unable to restrain himself from boasting. And there has to be enough time to pass the word.

"Still," she shrugged, "we have to try to do something to bring him down."

"I was thinking that maybe you took word yourself—riding down the back trail."

"You found that, then?" Bobbi said. "I thought you would. No, I never take that road. There's an armed camp at the foot of that trail, men posted there by Volker. Our cattle are allowed up if Volker has given his authorization. Otherwise, no one may travel up or down it."

"I see," Ty said thoughtfully. That canceled several ideas he had for finishing the outlaws. He was still wondering about Dahlia's part in all of this. "If your sister could be sure that you were safe, somehow, couldn't she just pack up and leave? Make a break for it?"

"You don't think Volker would track her down?" Bobbi asked, her eyes growing bitter. "He would find her wherever she ran. He is not a man who can stand to lose. Especially where it concerns her—that is what makes Dahlia's position doubly dangerous."

"I don't understand," Ty admitted.

"Really?" Bobbi showed surprise. "You're not the detective I thought you were, then. There's another man involved, Ty. Dahlia has a lover."

Ty was more puzzled than surprised. He frowned and asked, "You can't mean that big man with the mustache, Eric?"

Bobbi smiled. Her fingers remained on his arm as they spoke. "Then you didn't notice," she said. "It's funny, I thought the signs were too obvious. I suppose you had your thoughts on other matters, like Volker does. To a woman it would be apparent at a glance. No, not Eric. But the man was there the night you were, sleeping under the same roof."

Ty's head reeled with the thought. It couldn't be. He murmured the name. *"Champ!"*

"That's right," Bobbi confirmed. "Dahlia is crazy for Champ Studdard. Looking back, isn't it obvious?"

Ty supposed it was—if a man had been paying attention. The way Champ had kept his pony beside Dahlia all the way home as they rode guard. The way Champ had insisted that if he was going to die, he be taken to Dahlia's. The way she had worried over him, personally doctored Champ as they tried to patch him up. Would Dahlia do that for just any shot-up outlaw? He remembered her intent concentration as she operated, the deep relief on her face when she had finished and it seemed that Champ would recover.

"I guess it was pretty obvious, if a person knows," Ty admitted. "What about Volker?" he asked.

"He would kill them both in a heartbeat if he guessed it," Bobbi said.

"Yes, I suppose he would," Ty answered. They would have proven by their actions that they had no *loyalty* to Volker. "But Champ Studdard!"

"You mean, he's not much better? That he's an outlaw too, a killer?" Bobbi asked. Ty didn't reply. "Champ's story is a long and complicated one. I won't try to tell it for him," Bobbi said, continuing. "Like a lot of men of his time, he came back from the war to find his home burned, and his family dispersed by the Union army. He came west to

escape from the chaos in the south, from northern rule.
Those men—all any of them knew was fighting. They continued to use their guns on the frontier. Champ is an outlaw
through circumstance. I won't try to convince you or to
apologize for him. I don't know him that well, either. But
Dahlia believes in him. If you had been around Champ
more, you would have seen the vast difference between him
and a man like Volker, believe me."

Ty did not know the man, true, but he found himself almost believing Bobbi. He thought back to the day Champ
had stopped Corby from shooting George and possibly Ty
himself, then thrown him out of his outfit. Volker, on the
other hand, had tacitly given his blessing when Corby
wanted to gun down Spud. For the time being, Ty had neither to believe nor disbelieve Bobbi's assessment of
Champ. There were more urgent matters to attend to.

"Bobbi," he told her, "I need to get some information to
the Rangers. If I scribbled it out, could you get it to them
in Tucson?"

"I don't know," Bobbi had to answer honestly. "It all
depends on when Dahlia visits the ranch. How closely
we're being watched."

"But you could try?"

"I'll try, Ty. Anything that will help bring an end to
Volker's reign of terror is worth a try."

Ty smiled down at her and took the girl into his arms. It
was not too soon, he decided—not now—and he drew her
gently to him and kissed her.

Ty's information was scant and perhaps not vastly important, but he scrawled a note to Captain Payne telling him

what he did know. There were fifty outlaws in the group, under the command of a man calling himself Volker. At some time in the past he had called himself Mingo. The odds were very good that he was a former officer in the Southern army. It was also possible that he was known under that name or another in Tucson where he posed as a solid citizen. A brief description of Volker followed.

Also, Ty let him know, there was a back road to the valley, a seldom-used cattle trail, but it was guarded at its foot by an encampment of men loyal to Volker. The Shadow Riders had definitely been responsible for the raid of the freight line and the bank robbery at Titusville. Sperry and Michaels had been within spitting distance of the canyon trail two days earlier. If they retraced their route, they might be able to spot the entrance, but they would have to use extreme caution, as the trail was heavily guarded.

All in all it didn't seem like he was sending Ethan a lot of useful information, but it was more than the Rangers had learned previously, and some of it might prove useful in the long run.

Having written down his few comments, Ty folded the paper and passed the note to Bobbi for her safekeeping. He had mentioned nothing in the letter about Champ Studdard or Dahlia's house, an outlaw haven. Ty told himself that this was because he had run out of room on the page, but could not even convince himself that this was so.

A second, more lingering kiss served as their farewell, and as Bobbi rode away on her little paint pony, looking back at Ty, he considered that all in all he had managed to turn a day that had begun badly into a success. When he could no longer see Bobbi, he swung easily into the saddle of the borrowed gray horse, turned its head and started toward the home ranch, his heart much lighter than it had been in days.

Ty tugged his hat lower and let the stolid gray pick its way across the valley. He had much to think about, and much of it concerned the tiny woman with the wide brown eyes. He was less than an hour from the ranch, and he was looking forward to his first real meal in days, to the small comfort of his thin mattress.

The rifle shot rocketed across the distance and branded the gray horse's neck. Ty cursed his inattention, grabbed for his Winchester and kicked out of the stirrups to land roughly on the rocky ground and scamper toward a shallow wash, a second shot following him. The gray, startled, angry, tossed its head and stepped on its loose reins. Ty saw this only out of the corner of his eye.

He was watching for the rifleman.

Judd. Bobbi's cousin had seen them together when he came looking for the girl. Not over his grudge, he had found a place to lie in wait along the trail until a distracted Ty had ridden blithely past, then opened up with his Winchester.

Lifting his eyes above the rim of the gully, he peered through the loose screen of dry willow brush at the long, sunbright plain beyond. A third shot scored the earth too close for comfort, and he pressed himself down even more tightly against the dry earth.

He could not spot the sniper's position. The wind whipped away the gunsmoke as quickly as it blossomed from the man's weapon. He saw no muzzle flash. If he had, it might have been the last thing he ever saw anyway. The bullet already would have been sent on its deadly mission.

Ty knew that the shots had come from the west by their trajectory. The shooter, therefore, was clever enough to be firing from directly out of the setting sun, making detection even more difficult.

But that was all wrong! With the dense cover provided by the tangled growth in the big thicket, why would Judd circle the valley to find a place of concealment to the west? Ty's jaw tightened. It wasn't Judd who was doing the shooting.

Wynn Corby. It had to be. Although Ty had few friends among the outlaws, neither had he made any enemies. Except Corby. He cursed the day he had taken pity on the troubled young man and brought him to the outlaws' camp.

Another shot and then another dusted the rim of the wash near Ty's head. He ducked, covering his skull with his arm. This could not go on. Sooner or later through marksmanship or by chance one of those .44–40 slugs was going to find its target. He had to move.

Ty slid backward into the shallow wash. He began to run in a crouch, angling northward as the gully bottom ran, weaving through brush, leaping creekbed stones. The rifle fire followed him relentlessly. Spotting a stony outcropping ahead and to his right, Ty made for it, planning to use the solid rock as his bulwark. He was three strides from the shelter when a rifle bullet tore through his side, grazing the lowest rib and passed through, the depleted slug singing off the face of the outcropping. Ty tripped over his feet and went down, head spinning with the shock of pain.

Still dizzy, hot blood flowing from his wounded side, he crawled forward, rifle gripped firmly in hand, dragging himself behind the natural fortress. One more bullet pursued him, whining off solid stone to expend itself in the distance.

Then there was only silence. That and the hot seep of blood from his side, the pounding of tiny hammers in his head, the bother of gnats around his face, the disinterested golden eagle which still circled high above all human endeavors and concerns.

Ty rested his head against the stone. Sweat trickled from his forehead into his eyes. He wiped it away with the sleeve of his checkered shirt and then, facing the inevitability of it, he pulled the tail of his shirt up to examine the bullet wound. He could learn nothing he hadn't already suspected from a cursory look. Through muscle, front to back. Nicked the lowest rib. Bleeding like hell.

Unbuttoning his shirt he removed it painfully, wrapped it into a long dressing and tied it tightly around his waist to try to help stanch the blood flow.

The rifleman remained silent. The sun was slowly heeling toward the west. Already the lower half of its arc was lost behind the hills. Long, slow minutes passed. The shadows stretched out from beneath the rocks and the scattered brush. A covey of quail rushed past him along the gully floor, and doves cutting sharp silhouettes against the coloring sky flew home to roost. Ty smiled bitterly.

He was going to miss supper again.

When dusk had settled, purpling the land, when the

shadows had pooled and merged beneath the willows, Ty slid down from his rocky shelter to the floor of the gully, his side aching, burning with each movement. No shots followed him; it seemed the sniper had gone, surrendering to the darkness.

Ty found the gray horse not far along after he had succeeded in dragging himself out of the gully. The animal's ears twitched and it eyed him accusingly as he approached, but the gray stood for him to mount. Ty was glad that Tully had given him the patient older horse to ride that day. A wild-eyed flighty young mount like the palomino would have already run itself back to the home ranch, reins trailing.

It was full dark by the time Ty, leaning across the withers, doubled up with pain, holding his side with one hand, reached the ranch. Inside the barracks men were whooping it up, consuming a lot of raw whiskey. Tully was not celebrating, nor was the wrangler happy when, after helping Ty down from the gray's back, he found the narrow groove in the horse's flesh where the sniper's bullet had burned its neck. There was nothing to be said. Tully had seen far worse tending the outlaws' mounts, but the look he gave Ty was withering as he led the gray to the stable.

Ty made his way to the back kitchen door. There was fire in his blood and fire in his eyes. Without saying a word to Storch who sat at the plank table doing his figuring, or to the cook, Ty slammed his rifle down on the table, and, shirtless, stamped out the other door, his hand adjusting his Colt revolver in its holster.

Stalking to the other barracks through the deep shadows cast by the oak trees, Ty entered without knocking and demanded, "Where's Corby? Show him to me."

The first man to approach Ty along the aisle between the bunks where men sat sewing, cleaning their weapons, drinking, card playing, was Jake Skaggs himself.

"What's this all about?" the bearish man asked, his eyes taking in the shirtless man, the dirt on his face and body, the badly bandaged wound at once. "Who got you, Cannfield?" Skaggs asked.

"Corby. I need to see him," Ty said loudly. He still clutched his wounded side with one hand. His breath came in a panting cadence; his hair hung in his eyes.

"He's not here, Cannfield," Skaggs said shaking his head. "I sent a group out to relieve the canyon guards round about noon. Corby was one of them."

"Corby's not here?" Ty asked in disbelief. His voice had grown noticeably weaker. His head felt dizzy again. Skaggs shook his head heavily.

"He's been gone since noon, like I told you."

Then who . . . ? Ty mumbled an apology to Skaggs and stumbled out onto the porch, leaving the barracks door open. Someone closed it behind him and he found himself standing alone in the cool darkness of dusk. If not Corby, who had the sniper been? Who else had a motive? No one!

His eyes were drawn to the light burning in the window of the big house and a fragmentary thought flitted through his muddled mind. What if . . . what if the boss himself,

Volker, had happened to see Ty with Bobbi that afternoon? It could be that he would find it suspicious. It could be that he didn't like it one bit. There was no telling what the scarred man knew or feared might be true. Perhaps he just didn't like the idea of Ty cozying up with Dahlia's sister.

The thought was wispy, based on nothing at all, but it did give Ty one more possibility to consider as he staggered back to his barracks.

He ate his supper cold again and after having his wound tended to by the cook, dragged himself into his bunk where, hat over his face, he tried to sleep. Pain and worry did not allow sleep to come easily, and Ty was still awake long after the lanterns had been turned out and the outlaws had taken to their beds.

Around midnight a small, scuffling noise no louder than a mouse's scrabble caught his ear. Why the sound should have alerted him, he could not say, but it nudged something in the back of his mind and he rose from his bed. Shirtless, bandaged, he slipped out into the coolness of the night. He heard nothing above the chirping of the cicadas, the distant indistinct grumbling of some frogs, but he was suddenly aware of a moving shadow.

Beyond the oaks he thought he could discern a horse as black as midnight with a rider dressed in black making their slow way westward. Peering into the darkness, he tried to make out more details, but the shadowy figure disappeared into the night, merging with it like dream illusions. Frowning, Ty returned to his bunk where he lay staring up at the ceiling, unenlightened by what he had seen—or thought he had seen.

Three days later when Champ Studdard returned with Dahlia to take his place as the reigning casualty, Ty was feeling stronger, almost eager to ride. Champ was helped from Dahlia's buggy and walked to the bunkhouse amid much welcoming. His curiosity simmering, Ty forced himself to avoid watching the big house. Was Bobbi there to meet her sister or not? There was no telling, and with his thoughts as muddled as they were, Ty had no wish to arouse Volker's curiosity further.

Another night and day passed, and despite his body's returning strength, Ty felt impatient. He was annoyed with the situation and with himself.

He left the rowdy bunkhouse and walked slowly through the sun-dappled oaks, unsure if he was accomplishing anything, feeling that he knew nothing of importance, that all of this was a useless exercise. He felt drained, weary and totally inept.

In Phoenix, Captain Ethan Payne held a much more optimistic point of view. He read the telegram message from Chief Ranger Sam McGraw of their Tucson office. The information, delivered as usual by a Chinese who either did not speak or refused to speak English, had been promptly forwarded to Payne. It ran to two full yellow telegram pages. Payne read it through twice, dispatched his own answering wire to Tucson and summoned his clerk.

"Call in every man we have available, Ike. Are Sperry

and Michaels back yet? I want them if they are—and have them ready to travel within an hour."

"You're going . . . ?" the clerk inquired, his eyebrows drawing together.

"To Tucson. Things are heating up over there. I want to be there when all hell breaks loose."

Chapter Ten

"What I still don't understand," Ben Sperry was saying as the group of Arizona Rangers made their way south toward Tucson on a dew-bright morning, "is what convinces you that this is the time for us to break the backs of the Shadow Riders." Sperry was frowning. His long handlebar mustache rested firmly waxed across his upper lip. The long white silk scarf he always wore drifted in the early morning breeze.

Ethan laid it out for him. "It was in the telegram, Ben. Not the part that Cannfield wrote out, but in the short note McGraw tells me was scribbled on the back of it in another hand—a woman's by the look of it."

"I guess I wasn't paying that much attention," Sperry replied. "It meant nothing to me anyway. What was it? Something like 'New west spur A&E Sept. 30.'?"

"Exactly. You still have your memory, Ben."

"Maybe, Ethan. But maybe I'm losing my smarts. I didn't learn much from that bit of information."

"No? How about this: What is A&E?" Ben frowned more deeply and shrugged in response. Payne told him, "The Arizona & Eastern Railroad, Ben. They're opening a new railway spur to Yuma soon. I checked back with Sam McGraw, and he says . . ."

"That it's going into operation on the thirtieth," Sperry finished, the light having dawned. His frown did not lessen. "You think the outlaws are going to hit it on its initial run?"

"It's not what I think, Ben. It's 'Bert' who's telling us that it will happen."

"It's a big job . . . stopping a train. All those armed people on board," Sperry said thoughtfully.

"It is," Payne agreed. "How many men would it take, Ben?"

"Thirty, maybe? Fifty? . . . Oh, I get you now. Almost the entire outlaw force if they were going to do it right."

"Almost all," Payne agreed. "But it would be worth it if they could pull it off. There'll be gold on board. Plus all of the railroad dignitaries and important citizens of both Tucson and Yuma and their wives who will undoubtedly break out all their jewelry to compete with each other."

Sperry touched his waxed mustache thoughtfully. "It would be a big haul, all right. If you had the men to handle it." He added, "In a way you've got to hand it to him— he's got gall."

"Who's that, Ben?"

"Well . . . I guess we're calling him Volker."

"Volker, yes," Payne agreed. "It seems he's tired of these small jobs and wants to end his career with one big bang."

"Seems to me," Sperry commented, "that stopping the train itself is the biggest part of a job like this. I mean, you can't just wreck it, can't count on the engineer stopping just because you wave a pistol at him. You'd have to find where it slowed on a long upgrade. Or . . ."

"Or maybe where it had to stop for fuel or water," Payne suggested.

"That would work, but that would mean townspeople crowded around as well, wouldn't it?"

"Not necessarily, Ben. The line is new. There aren't many settlements along the route as of yet. There happens to be a collection of mostly abandoned ramshackle buildings fifty miles along the line. A nameless spot on the map where the railroad has constructed a new water tower."

"You're kidding? That would be a natural. Buildings for the raiders to hide in, no local population, no lawmen around." Ben Sperry considered this information. "How would the outlaws even know of such a place, know that the train would have to stop there? Unless there was an inside man. Someone who knew the details of the railroad's plan. I mean, this is the inaugural run, right? Who could know what their plan was otherwise?"

"I think they had a way," Captain Payne said. "McGraw has provided another tidbit of information that I found interesting. When the line was being laid out, the railroad needed to hire local surveyors, men who knew the territory better than their regular staff. By coincidence there was a surveyor located directly across the street from their own new Tucson office."

"Don't tell me . . ."

"It seems the surveyor was a man who had been in town for six months or so. He wasn't in his office much, spending days on end out working in the desert, settling mining claims, land disputes and all. Seldom seen, but well-known. A man named Richard Volker."

Ben cursed silently, savagely enough to cause his enormous waxed mustache to twitch. "That took some planning," Ben said at length. "I gave the man credit for having gall. Now I guess I have to give him credit for having some brains to go along with it. But, Nathan, if all this is true—and I don't doubt it—how could our friend 'Bert' have learned anything about it? As smart as he is, Volker wouldn't be free with that information. Only he and one or two important and trustworthy men could have known. Maybe the men who scouted out the town with the new water tank." Ben waited for an answer, but Captain Payne had none for him.

"That's something we won't learn until after this is finished. The important thing is that we have the chance to trap the entire band, or most of it, outside their stronghold. The army's been notified, of course—even if we could muster every ranger in the territory, we wouldn't have enough of our own men for this action." Payne raised a hand to still an objection by Sperry. "I didn't go directly to Colonel Toomey at Camp Grant—damned old fool—I wired General Crook himself. Let's see Toomey ignore that directive!"

"How many soldiers are you asking for, Ethan?"

"All of them! Every man they don't need to stand guard on the post. We're going to stop Volker when he jumps the train, stop him cold. Then we're going after their home camp. We'll use the back trail Cannfield has reported. If there's an outlaw settlement at the foot of it—well, they won't be enough to stand off a company of cavalry. At the same time we'll attack the canyon trail, not with the idea of actually rushing it, but to make them believe that we are so they'll bring all available guns to that side of the valley.

"We'll get them, Ben. One way or another Volker is finished."

They rode in silence for another half a mile, beginning the descent toward Tucson across the long hills. Ben broke the silence to ask the question that had been nagging him. "Does Camfield know about Volker?" he asked.

Ethan understood the question. "No. And he mustn't find out now. It would ruin everything."

"You already knew about him when you recruited Ty, Ethan."

"Not exactly, Ben. I knew about Mingo, yes. If you remember, for a while we didn't even have that name tied up with that band of Texas Comancheros. It wasn't until Ty was gone that we discovered who Mingo was. When we went for him, he had fled. Moved to Arizona where he continued his depredations. By the time you and I came out to the territory, I knew who Mingo was, what he had done.

"But I did not know about Volker, didn't realize that he and Mingo were one and the same. You're right, I didn't tell Ty everything we knew about the man we suspected of being the leader of the Shadow Riders. How could I have told him, Ben? What do you think Ty would have done if he had learned that we had discovered that it was definitely Mingo who killed Kathleen back in Texas?"

"I understand, and you were probably right in doing what you did," Sperry agreed reluctantly. "Still it seems . . ."

"Deceitful? Treacherous?" Ethan suggested. "Ben, the plan was in place. I needed a desperate, canny man for the job. I had to think of my obligation to the territory first. Ty will be told. One day."

"I don't want to be around when you have to tell him that you knew all along who his wife's killer was," Ben said. He wagged his head heavily. "What makes a man like Mingo anyway? How many women did he confess to killing? Six?"

"Six. Yes. Mingo must be insane, plain crazy is all I can figure, Ben. There's a reason that he hates women, but I'm not smart enough to figure out what it is. Apparently he treats them like angels at first, showering them with gifts and finery, and then when things go wrong he takes it out on them. I don't pretend to understand it. I only hope that we are able to take him down before he can harm another one . . ."

"Ethan!" Ben remembered suddenly. "On the back of that note the Chinese delivered to McGraw. The writing. You said that it was a woman's writing."

"Yes," Ethan answered, "it was in a woman's hand." He could only hope that whoever she was, the lady could run fast and far before the outlaw's plans were thwarted. Because he knew that losing could send Mingo into another of his frenzies. And he would almost certainly strike out against her in savage rage.

Six was enough. Ethan did not think he could stand being responsible for number seven.

Ty had not had the chance to see Bobbi, to find out if his message to the Rangers had gotten out. The word to the men in the outlaw camp now was to "stay close and stay ready." Something big was up, but no one knew what it was, and of course no one was asking. There was more than the usual amount of restlessness in camp. Fistfights broke out more frequently; the grumbling was louder. Complaints were often silenced when someone would remind the griper "What do you care if nothing's happening? You're making more money every passing day for just sitting on your rump."

But the frequent rejoinder heard was, "Yeah, but what is there to spend it on? Money's no good if all you can do is count it."

Some of the complaining crew—like Beech, a man with tightly curled red hair and an unusually long nose whom Studdard had suspected of being ready to run with his share of gold after the freight office stickup—were even more rebellious as the days of inactivity slowly passed.

Ty heard the gripes of Beech and others like him, but none of the outlaws would ever rat on their fellow raiders, even when the talk went beyond simple complaints. Ty was outside on the porch in front of the barracks, chair tilted back against the wall, when he got an earful through an open window.

"There's the back road," Beech was saying convincingly to a group gathered around his bunk. "What's to keep us from loading our saddlebags with what gold we've got and heading out? There's women and good times to be had somewhere, and me, I figure I deserve some of it."

"It's a thought," replied a second man, one Ty recognized by his slight stutter to be an outlaw named Chipper. "Who's to stop us? The boys sure wouldn't ride us down."

"Yeah," a third man said lazily, "but have you considered that one day, no matter if you was to ride to Mexico, you might look up one day and find the man standing over you with a gun? Not for me, thanks."

Ty wished to hear no more. He rose, stretched and walked across the yard and into the scattered shade of the wind-shifted oaks. He was only a little surprised to meet another man there. Champ, wearing a lime-green shirt, blue jeans and his ever-present Stetson with its silver band, was leaning on a cane, watching the trickle of a stream that ran whispering through the grove. He looked up as Ty entered the small, leaf-littered clearing.

"Mornin', Ty, How's the side?" Champ asked.

"Just about healed. How're you doing?"

"Much better," Champ replied, his eyes briefly lifting to watch a meadowlark wing away. "I can even ride some. Getting up on a horse is no fun, but once on, it's not too bad. I went out for a short stretch this morning."

Ty said nothing though he was curious. Why would

Champ be riding, and where? Just to see if he could, was the simple answer, and Ty supposed that the order to "stay close" did not necessarily apply to an outlaw of Champ's rank.

"Is Beech still at it?" Champ asked as if he had been reading Ty's mind.

"I suppose," Ty replied vaguely.

"You'd think the man would have more sense. You know how the boss feels about loyalty. He wouldn't stand for it."

"No, I guess he wouldn't." Ty refused to be drawn out on the subject. Besides, he took it all just to be bunkhouse talk among restless men. On the other hand, there were numbers of questions that he would like to have asked Champ after his last conversation with Bobbi, but these seemed to go beyond the boundary. Champ turned and faced Ty, his dark eyes cautionary, searching.

"Needn't tell anyone, Ty, but something is about to happen. Something big. There's to be a meeting tonight to lay it out. The boss, Skaggs, Dink and me will be there. You'll be sent for."

Ty nodded. He was still in, then. Did that mean that Mingo was not the man who had been shooting at him the other day? He didn't spend much time trying to figure it out. Trying to understand what was going on around the outlaw camp had brought him little success. Perhaps tonight things would come clearer.

"One thing," Champ said in a lowered voice. "Your old friend Corby will be there too. Don't ask me how, but he has convinced Skaggs that he's tough and reliable. Or maybe the boss had a hand in it, but Corby's been promoted to lieutenant under Skaggs. Whatever's between you two, you'll have to keep a lid on it." Champ's voice carried a quiet warning. "It will be better for the both of you to cooperate, Ty."

Ty nodded his understanding. Champ half-smiled and started on his way, leaning heavily on his cane as he trudged across the fallen oak leaves. Ty watched the outlaw go. Frowning, he decided that he knew less day by day. How had Corby managed to climb back out of the pit he had dug for himself? What was the big job that was being planned?

Slowly making his way back toward the barracks, scattering the three mangy dogs that were camp hangers-on, he considered the situation, and his own predicament. Hearing voices raised in argument from the barracks, he considered leaking the word that a big job was very close, that there would soon be plenty of action. Or a warning that the boss had heard rumors of Beech's talk. Either of these might be seen as a breach of confidence, however, and he decided against it.

Ty walked around the end of the building toward the barn to see to his sorrel. The silent, trusting company of the big animals housed there seemed preferable to the human kind. Bill Cox and George Hubler, always together, were in front of the barn, Cox on a bench whittling, Hubler crouched down playing a solo game of mumblety-peg. Ty lifted a hand, said a few words of greeting and passed by.

Entering the barn he saw the sorrel lift its head eagerly and shudder, it glossy flesh quivering. The horse was ready to be out and moving again. Ty slipped inside the paddock and began currying the sorrel. His hands moved automatically; his thoughts were far away.

There was always the back road, as Beech had pointed out. What if he were simply to ride out? What if he happened to find Bobbi out there, or at her house? Suppose he could talk her into riding away with him, simply leaving the valley behind? It could be done, he supposed. Even if there was an encampment of watching outlaws below, the settlement could probably be skirted, or passed in the night . . .

"Do horses dream?" Ty asked the sorrel with some bitterness. The horse twitched an ear and stamped his white-stockinged forefoot, wanting the brushing to continue.

Bobbi would never agree. She had too much loyalty to Dahlia, to her father's memory to give up now. It would be cowardice to her, he knew. And that was what it would be for Ty. He had given his word to Captain Payne, promised to stick it out, and in a way, that vow had been given to all of the people of Arizona Territory. It was another sort of loyalty that was required of Ty, and he could not turn his back on his oath either. Placing the currycomb on its nail, Ty went out again, gloomier than ever.

It was nightfall before the messenger came to summon Ty to the big house. He grabbed his hat and left, not pausing to answer any of the questions in the eyes of the gathered outlaws. The meeting took place not in the boss' office, but in a large room Ty had not entered before, a sort of parlor with blue-velvet chairs and a long mahogany table. A huge painting of a stag hunt was hung above a white-brick fireplace with brass andirons. Was this where Dahlia was entertained on her visits? Ty wondered.

There was a silver tray on the table with a cut-glass decanter filled with dark liquor. Those present had already poured themselves drinks. Big Jake Skaggs was there, as were a sullen Corby, Dink and Champ who alone was resting in a chair, his cane positioned between his knees. Ty wasn't offered a drink; he did not take one. There was no general conversation; they only waited tensely.

Mingo entered the room a few minutes later, his eyes darting to each of them in turn. He acknowledged their presence with a curt nod and immediately got down to business.

"Make your men ready for a night ride, gentleman," Volker said without preliminaries. Ty thought he could detect a note of nervousness even in the boss' voice. "The moon will be rising just before eleven. Have your soldiers at the top of the pass, ready to ride it by midnight."

He told them nothing of the purpose of the night excursion. Perhaps that was only for Volker and his two top lieutenants to know. Ty was surprised when Volker's snake eyes settled on his own and locked with them.

"You have been to the water tower before, Cannfield. You'll serve as guide for Dink's company."

The water tower? What water tower? Then Ty recalled the scouting expedition Champ had taken Corby and himself on. The tiny outpost with its scattered tumbledown buildings. And a water tower, which had seemed odd at the time, not belonging there.

"Corby," Volker said, shifting away toward Corby who

stood drinking his whiskey, his eyes still dark with emotion. "You've been there, too. You'll guide Skaggs' crew."

There, Ty thought, was an explanation for Corby being invited to the meeting, for his sudden advancement. Corby only nodded. His eyes the entire time were fixed on Ty, not on Volker.

"I can ride," Champ offered quietly. "Don't you think it's better if I lead my men?"

"I don't want you riding," Volker snapped. "You're not fit and you know it!"

Champ shrugged using one shoulder and an upturned hand. He took another sip from his whiskey glass and fell silent. Volker had withdrawn a gold watch from his vest pocket. He snapped it open, nodded to himself, and closed the timepiece again.

"You've got three hours. I want every man, his weapons and his horse ready at moonrise."

"You're not going?" Dink asked. The flabby man's question seemed odd. So far as Ty knew, Volker never rode with his men on these raids. He half-expected Volker to flare up in anger at being questioned. Instead he smiled and answered, "No. However, I may meet you there."

What did that mean? Ty wondered. And what could be so big that the entire outlaw rank was needed to pull it off? Fifty armed men were enough to tree a town, but such recklessness was not a keynote of Volker's methods.

No further information was offered; no other questions were asked. Volker left the room first, and Ty followed shortly after, leaving the others to their whiskey.

Outside it was full dark. The stars were plentiful and

bright but they did little to illuminate the dark earth as Ty made his way back toward the barracks. He had taken only half a dozen steps when he heard the sounds of movement behind him, and he turned sharply, thinking of Corby and his apparently endless hate of Ty.

The night held no danger, however. What Ty had heard was a man leading a horse. It was Volker's house man, the guard he had first heard blurt out Mingo's name, angering the boss. The horse he led was one Ty thought he had seen before. It was black as coal without a single white hair to mar its Satanic appearance. The house man did not notice Ty standing there in the darkness, and he continued on his way, leading the horse toward the back of the house where Volker had his office and his private quarters. Ty watched until he could see man and horse no longer, then continued on his way.

The night was once again crowded with too many mysteries to comprehend.

Chapter Eleven

The outlaw army moved in darkness down the steep twisting pass toward the desert floor below. The moon silvered rocky outcroppings and left the crevices in darkness. No one spoke as the horses cautiously picked their way along the trail where a misstep could send rider and mount plummeting down the sheer precipice to the canyon bottom. Occasionally a horse blew. Now and then a man muttered a curse. Saddle leather creaked and bridle chains chinked softly. There was no conversation.

The outlaws had complained that they were weary of inactivity, ready to ride, but when they had been roused for a midnight foray, there was nothing but loud complaining among them in the bunkhouse and in the stable as they mounted. The group of men led by Dink and Ty reached the foot of the trail first and rested their mounts in the staging area, the dry-grass valley. They had arrived first and would move out onto the desert first. If one of the groups happened to be spotted and intercepted, the other would still have a chance of making it through to their destination.

One other distinction separated Ty and Dink's band from that of Skaggs. Skaggs' men had done their saddling in the enclosure where the army bay horses were kept, and each of the outlaws under Skaggs' command had been issued army uniforms, some of them mismatched and worn, some as crisp as the day they had been issued—all previously worn by the army deserters. These men all had army experience, and Ty thought they looked as disciplined, and no more ragtag than any regular desert army unit.

Ty stood holding the reins to his sorrel, studying the night and the blank distances of the desert beyond as they waited for stragglers. The stars were bright beyond the glow of the rising moon, the white desert marked by occasional shadows cast by sage or stands of creosote bushes. Nothing moved across its broad face.

But Ty continued to watch and wonder. He had been among the first to emerge from the canyon into the clearing. As he had dismounted he had become aware of something that should not be there. He could smell the faintest hint of dust lingering in the air, and it seemed that he could make out the barest trace of sand sifting down as if there had been a rider out before them who was now making his solitary way across the desert toward Tucson.

"Let's get moving," Dink said in a low growl, and Ty nodded to the fleshy outlaw, swinging aboard to take his position at the point of the command, to guide them toward who-knew-what blood spectacle Volker had designed for them.

"How about the army?" Michaels asked, not with worry, but with understandable concern.

"Colonel Toomey sent a courier," Captain Payne told him. "They're camped half an hour east of town."

There were four men gathered in Chief Ranger Sam Mc-Graw's Tucson office. McGraw himself—narrow, glassy-eyed, his mouth a fixture for his stubby pipe, Ethan Payne and his two right-hand men, Ben Sperry with his waxed mustache, dapper clothing and long white silk scarf and Cope Michaels who was nearly Sperry's opposite in dress and demeanor. Cope looked as if he had just escaped from some desert hellhole where his buckskin shirt and torn Levi's had been scrounged from a rag bin. If he had lain unmoving on the desert, it was unlikely anyone would have noticed him, taking him for a dead animal. His face was decorated with a longish graying beard growing in all directions. Behind appearances, Cope was quick and intelligent.

"How many of our men have arrived?" Sperry asked.

"Fourteen is all, unless some more drag in before dawn," Payne told him. "And they'll drag in dead tired, not good for much."

"How many are you gong to put on the train?" Cope asked.

"Only five or six—we don't want to give the game away. Someone could be watching." Payne allowed himself a smile despite the seriousness of the situation. He told

Sperry lightly, "We're going to have to steal a little of your thunder, Ben."

"I don't get you, Captain."

"That scarf of yours. Tell McGraw here why you wear it."

"The scarf? It started when I was a youngster, scouting for the army in the Dakotas. In the early days some of those men wore their hair long on purpose, to taunt the Indians, saying 'Here's my lovely scalp, but you can't have it.' I started wearing the scarf for about the same reason—I was a cocksure kid in those days. I was saying 'Here comes Ben Sperry, but there ain't a warrior among you who can take me down.'"

McGraw had been listening silently. Now he removed his pipe from his mouth long enough to say, "I've already seen to it, Ethan."

Sperry and Michaels both looked puzzled. Captain Payne enlightened them. "The same as Sam used to wear the white scarf to identify himself, we're going to issue them to all of our rangers so that they can't be mistaken for the enemy. There's going to be a hell of a lot of confusion out there to-morrow; I don't want any man shot by mistake. We all wear white scarves to identify ourselves."

"It's an idea," Sperry agreed. Then, more thoughtfully he looked at Ethan and asked, "Captain, who's going to issue a scarf to Ty Cannfield?"

Sunrise brought the glow of scarlet and gold to the eastern sky. The flanks of the mountains, still lost in shadow, turned to deep purple. A roadrunner crossed the silver railroad tracks, paused as if in surprise and raced by on spindly legs. Sweat was already trickling into Ty's eyes and he removed his hat to mop his brow with his blue bandana. He was sitting his sorrel pony on the low ridge rising behind the abandoned town where the railroad engineers had decided to build the new water tower, perhaps thinking that the town could reinvent itself as a depot once the trains began to run.

The eyes of the men along the ridge were fixed on the rail line. No matter how a man tried to distract his attention, his gaze constantly returned to the long thin lines of steel which seemed to run away to infinity. Watching, waiting for a puff of smoke, the distant shrilling of a steam whistle, the onrushing clank of the locomotive. Ty's band of outlaws grew impatient, constantly adjusting masks, rechecking the loads in their guns. Below, in the shanty town, all was silent. A dozen men were concealed inside the ramshackle buildings there, waiting to do their part.

Across the tracks, to the south, hidden in a deep sandy wash, Skaggs and his army of uniformed men waited as impatiently. After the first strike, to be launched against the train by Dink and his outlaws, the job of the "army" Skaggs commanded was to ride to the rescue of the passengers and crew of the train. These, presumably, would come out to welcome their rescuers and could then be easily disarmed and held at gunpoint as Dink's band of men returned to finish the job.

That was Volker's plan according to Dink, and Cannfield could find no flaws in it. Even if by some remote chance the false army Skaggs led was exposed for what it was, still the outlaws had a large enough number of men to finish the job, although the blood toll would soar much higher if it came to an all-out battle.

Ty had been searching his mind for a way to warn the train crew, to halt the attack, but there was none. Even if the engineer on the train were alerted, his locomotive could not run much farther without taking on water, and it would die out on the desert, the additional pursuit being only an inconvenience to the Shadow Riders.

The sound, when it came, was eerie, high-pitched like the sound of a screech owl, distant and melancholy, rolling across the desert to die against the distant hills. All eyes shifted toward the sound of the locomotive's whistle, blaring its way westward.

"Get ready," Dink muttered unnecessarily. They were all ready, had been since midnight, since dawn, since the day they had chosen the outlaw trail. Masks were drawn up, rifles unlimbered. Ty, peering eastward, saw the tiny dot on the horizon. It quickly became a smudge of smoke and the gleam of sunlit bright metal. Within minutes he could make out the distinctive shape of the locomotive's diamond smokestack, breathing torrents of white smoke. Then the long train became visible in its entirety. Brightly painted freight cars, green Pullmans, the red caboose.

"Start on down," Dink said loudly, nervously. The flabby outlaw was feeling the strain of command, the anxiousness of battle. Ty had tied his own bandana across his face. He rode forward as the others did. There was no choice to be made. How, though, was he supposed to survive the battle without shooting innocent men? Failing to do so would lead to immediate discovery, and probable assassination at the hands of the Shadow Riders themselves. His choice then was death at the hand of strangers—or death at the hand of those he rode with.

The men hidden in the shacks below had also been alerted. Ty now saw the doors to the huts being opened. Other outlaws hidden behind the shacks stood with their rifles ready. He could see nothing of the uniformed men across the tracks. They were well-hidden, and Skaggs was keeping their impulse to attack under control.

But what was that to the east? Ty frowned, squinted into the brightness of the rising sun. He thought he saw a moving veil of dust, believed he saw a few small specks of color, but he could not be sure and as they descended the flank of the hills, whatever he had seen was lost behind the ridge. He could only hope it was help arriving, knowing that whoever it might be, whatever their plan, much blood was still going to flow on this morning. Dink glanced back at him to discover why he was hesitating and Ty kneed the sorrel ahead to catch up.

I may meet you there.

Those had been Volker's words on the night before. *How, when? Could it be that Volker himself was leading another band of men in from the east? Where could he have assembled them? No, that wasn't Volker that Ty had seen. Probably it was someone who had no part in the raid at all. A herd of cattle on the move, freight wagons, westbound settlers . . .*

The train whistle bleated again, this time near enough that its shrill exhalation was startling. Ty glanced that way, saw the locomotive roaring toward them, felt rather than saw that it was slowing. His last hope gone—that the train might continue on, rolling at full speed past the ambushers—Ty took up his position in the shadows of a falling-down building and waited for the deep voices of the guns to begin speaking.

Bill Cox and George Hubler were near Ty. There was perspiration on Bill's forehead. George's good eye was narrowed in concentration, studying the approaching train. Dink had taken up a position nearer the water tank. He was crouched down now, rifle across his knee. There was no stopping the battle to come, no way to avoid a massacre. Fifty men waited, guns at the ready for the crew and passengers on the train. Desperation more than inspiration set Ty into motion.

"It's not going to stop!" he shouted to Cox. Ty was swinging onto his sorrel pony.

Bill's eyes narrowed in puzzlement. "It's slowing down, Ty!"

"It's not going to stop. Listen to what I'm telling you, Bill! I've got to get to the locomotive. I'll damn sure stop it. Tell Dink what I'm doing!"

Before Bill could respond, Ty had spun the sorrel around and was now racing past the astonished outlaws toward the train tracks. Bill, after a moment's indecision, rushed toward Dink, running in a crouch.

"Tell everybody to hold their fire! Ty's going to stop the train."

Dink was paralyzed by indecision. The fat bandit lieutenant rose to his feet, watched the vanishing sorrel horse carry Ty eastward. Men looked to Dink for instructions. Still uncertain, Dink called out, "Hold your fire! It's Cannfield stopping the train."

Given time to think it over, Dink became concerned. Ty's rash act was upsetting the scheme of things. What did Cannfield know that he didn't? In another minute it would make no difference. Ty was nearly out of rifle range even if they'd had a logical reason to shoot him.

"He'd better stop that train now," Dink said under his breath. "He'd damn sure better."

The fireman stood on the swaying platform of the tender, wiping his brow. He had been shoveling coal for only an hour or so, but under the desert sun it became hot work early. The engineer was peering out from the side of the locomotive cab, watching for the landmark water tower. At the same time both men became aware of a man on a frothing sorrel horse riding beside the locomotive. Had the train been at full speed he would have had no chance of catching up. Now with the locomotive slowing, his long-legged pony had just enough speed for the stranger to pull even, grab the iron rail next to the locomotive cab steps and leap from his saddle onto the train.

"Who the hell are you?" the engineer, a thick, brusque man demanded.

"Trouble," Ty told him, unholstering his Colt and drawing back the hammer. "Keep this thing rolling! Get some speed under it."

"The hell I will," the engineer shot back.

"Have it your way, but I'll have to shoot you if you don't," Ty said and his eyes said he meant it. To the fireman, Ty

shouted, "Get shoveling. Get a full head of steam up again."
He looked ahead toward the collection of shacks and the
new water tower appearing much larger now; still no outlaws were visible.

"We have to have water!" The fireman said in consternation. "You know what will happen to that boiler if it
runs dry?"

"You know what will happen to you if you don't do like
I say?" Ty said, shifting the muzzle of his pistol toward the
fireman who scrambled to the door of the tender furnace,
opened it and began furiously shoveling coal into the fire-
box. "Open up that throttle," Ty said to the engineer. "All
the way!"

"It'll blow!"

"Let it blow. Just so it gets us a few more miles down the
tracks. Dammit, man, don't you understand? Outlaws—
ready to jump us at the water stop!"

"This is the end of my job with A&E," the engineer
complained, and he opened the throttle wide. Immediately the locomotive gave a lurch forward and within minutes, Ty could feel that their speed was greatly increasing.

A man with a shotgun held loosely in one hand
leaped from the roof of the freight car behind the tender
and landed roughly on the platform. Ty swung around
to brace him, but was met with a grin from the familiar
face.

"Sperry!"

"It's me, Cannfield," Ben said. The wind whipped his
white scarf around his neck. "There's six of us on board.
Ethan's following with the main party. We've got soldiers

coming too. Where are they waiting?" he asked as they approached the water tower at thirty miles an hour.

Sperry had no need to wait for an answer. In the next moment a dozen guns opened up from beside and within the dilapidated buildings of the abandoned town and another dozen charged the train on horseback. Sperry and Ty ducked low behind the iron plate of the locomotive cab. Lead banged off the inch-thick steel harmlessly. The engineer, now operating his throttle from a crouch, shot a wildly fearful glance which might have contained mingled thanks at Ty.

Sperry yelled above the roar of the locomotive. "Their horses won't be able to keep up! Any others around?"

"Twenty or so dressed as soldiers," Ty said, pointing to the other side of the tracks. Sperry scuttled that way to peer over the iron bulwark.

"I see them," Sperry said. "They're not going to catch up either."

"The hell they're not," the engineer said in a snarl. Studying his gauges, he told them, "We've got three, maybe five miles left until we're out of water, out of steam. Then the boiler's going to blow. If they've got good ponies under them, they'll catch us!"

"Can you see Ethan's rangers?" Ty asked, ignoring the engineer's complaint as he edged up beside Sperry.

"No. Don't forget we're leaving them behind as well."

Ty was able to make out the sharp reports of half a dozen rifles above the racket of the train, and as he watched one of the outlaws dressed as a soldier dropped from his horse to roll across the sand. Another man veered away from the pursuit, his pony limping horribly. The rangers riding the train were finding their marks—but it wouldn't be enough to convince Skaggs or Dink to pull back. Too much was riding on this.

The boiler issued a pained, iron-bellied sound. The engineer looked desperate. He fiddled with his valves, but nothing worked. Already they were beginning to lose speed. Already the pursuing horsemen seemed nearer.

"We have no chance," the engineer said dismally.

"Wait!" Sperry said. He was pointing to the low hills flanking the north side of the tracks. "Look up there, Ty!"

Ty saw them now. A line of blue-shirted horsemen cresting the dark rise. Colonel Toomey's cavalry from Camp Grant had been positioned in just the right place. There was no way that the army force could mount a charge against the outlaws and hope to catch them, but they were able now to open fire effectively from that distance and, looking out the other side of the locomotive cab, Ty saw three Shadow Riders shot from their saddles. The trouble was complicating itself: The longer the train managed to keep running, the more distance it put between itself and the outlaws on their tiring mounts; however, the longer the locomotive held together, the farther the train was from the army contingent and the pursuing Arizona Rangers.

"Hope you're carrying a lot of ammo," Sperry muttered. "It's going to get ugly, Ty."

Again Ty considered that the only chance they had was if the outlaws gave up their pursuit. He knew they would not, could not give up the chase. He had done all he could and it wasn't enough.

The next instant the locomotive boiler blew sky high.

One moment the train was rumbling along at breakneck speed, devouring the miles of silver rail under its great iron wheels; the next a huge explosion from the boiler's bowels ripped through the locomotive, staggering it in its tracks. Red flame and smoke spewed into the air. Boiler plate and rivets were blown across the desert. Shrapnel banged off the locomotive cab and they ducked to avoid the flying missiles. Scalding steam escaped from a burst line and the fireman screamed in pain as his legs were badly burned.

"Let's go!" Ty said. They were exposed where they now stood. They had to make their way back to the passenger cars, to fort up and wait for help to arrive—if it could arrive in time. Ty and Sperry hooked the injured fireman under either arm and scrambled to the ground, the engineer in their wake. Running for their lives, they avoided any bullets the distant raiders fired at them, made it to the first Pullman car, and dragging the burned railroad man between them, clambered aboard.

A man with a rifle in one hand rushed to help them. Ty noticed that he had a white scarf around his neck. Sperry grinned. "All the good guys have those. Ethan's idea."

Ty nodded. They helped the fireman into a seat and moved the length of the car in a crouch, past big-bellied bankers and railroad men with their pistols drawn, their ladies dripping expensive jewelry, a few frightened inaugural passengers who now deeply regretted their ticket purchases.

"Get back to the second car, Ben," Ty ordered. "Tell the people there to tear up the seat cushions and use them as best they can to barricade the windows—that'll keep the glass from flying at least."

"Right," Sperry said and then he was gone, still moving in a crouch. Ty found a big man with a gold chain across his bulging belly who seemed to be in charge and told him, "Any soldiers coming from the south are outlaws. Those to the north are real troops from Camp Grant. The Arizona Rangers are coming too—they'll all be wearing white silk scarves. Mind your targets."

"I am Allison Steele of the Arizona & Eastern Railroad," the big man said, puffing up. "May I inquire who you are?"

"I'm the man who just blew up your train," Ty answered. "Just do what I tell you and pass the word on who's who out there. It's confusing enough as things stand without us shooting at our own people."

Conversation abruptly became a pointless exercise. Gunfire from north and south erupted in savage volleys. A hailstorm of lead rang off the Pullman's metalwork; within a minute there was not a window in the car unbroken. The women were forced to the floor to find what shelter they could as the few rangers and the untrained businessmen returned fire.

Packed as closely together as they were, with horses panicked by the guns, the attacking Shadow Riders began to take casualties even against this feeble resistance. Ty saw a masked outlaw in an army uniform be dragged away, his boot hooked through the stirrup of his retreating horse's saddle.

Caught in the chaos, Ty tried to pick his targets carefully rather than fire blindly as some of the passengers were doing. From the corner of his eye which was focused down the sight of his Winchester, Ty saw Allison Steele get hit in the shoulder, saw a woman's mouth open wide in a protest that could not be heard above tumult, saw another passenger hit in the right arm, the bullet leaving it dangling, bloody.

Ty settled his sights on one of the leaders of the fake cavalry and squeezed off a shot. He recognized the man as his mask fell from his face. Jake Skaggs himself took the .44 bullet from Ty's rifle through the chest and tumbled from his pony. The charging horses stampeded past his body, most managing to avoid him, but two or three of the animals pressed together tightly as they trampled him.

Still there was no sign of the Rangers' main body. The troops from Camp Grant were reluctant to charge, it seemed. They held back, sniping at Dink's body of men from the foot of the hills. Mentally, Ty urged them to mount, to advance, and for Captain Payne and the Rangers to catch up with the disabled train.

If the Rangers could not catch up—Ty thought as he saw yet another passenger go down to lie unmoving against the aisle of the Pullman car—very few were going to make it off this train alive.

Bullets by the hundreds continued to puncture the bodywork of the Pullman and two more men were injured or killed. Hunkered down, Ty fired over the sill of the window. An incoming bullet ricocheted angrily off the steel, inches from his wrist. Each time he raised his head to fire he was met with a fusillade of bullets from the raiders who had now reached the train and simply sat their milling horses, cutting loose at any target that presented itself.

The train sat like a dying serpent against the silver tracks. The outlaw guns continued to blaze away in staccato fury. Ty was risking death each time he lifted his eyes to return fire. Still no relief force had arrived. Matters could get no worse. And then they did.

Above the veil of drifting gunsmoke it was difficult to pick out the fire-scent at first, but then Ty detected it. He glanced toward the rear of the train and saw the plume of darker smoke oozing into the car from beneath the door. The faint glow of heated burning wood could be seen at the door's upper edge.

The train was on fire.

Chapter Twelve

"**W**e're on fire!" Ty called to Allison Steele. The wounded, disheveled railroad magnate looked up at Ty with furious eyes.

"They're trying to burn us alive! The savages!"

Ty doubted that the outlaws had done it intentionally before they had the chance to loot the train. It was more likely that embers from the boiler explosion had started the fire, but it didn't matter what had started it. People had to be moved, and quickly. The flames could now be seen clearly, tiny fans of fire licking at the rear wall of the Pullman.

"We've got to cross into the next car," Ty told Steele. "Move them as swiftly as you can. Try to keep everyone calm. We don't need a stampede."

"All right," Steele said, thrusting his .36 Remington behind his broad belt. This was a task the businessman seemed well suited for. Used to giving commands and having them obeyed, he had the women on their feet, the passengers patiently waiting their turns as the door of the Pullman was opened and frantic word passed to the car behind them that they were coming through. Ty took up a position at the rear window of the burning car and laid down a withering fire in hopes of protecting the fleeing passengers as they crossed between the two cars. He levered through a full magazine of shots, firing until the barrel of his Winchester was hot. How many men he hit, how many killed, he could not tell, but closely packed as they were, surely a few of the attacking men and horses were taken out of action.

The first man Ty met as he leaped across the space between the two Pullman cars was Ben Sperry, his mustache still waxed to perfection. His eyes however were pained, his shirt torn. "Any point in trying to uncouple from the burning cars?" he asked as Ty banged the door shut behind him.

"No. We have no way of putting distance between us. Where's Ethan?"

"I wish I knew. He should have been here by now . . . unless those tricky dogs laid an ambush for him along the trail."

"They didn't," Ty said, but he was not so sure. No one but Volker, it seemed, ever knew all of his plans.

And then, with that thought still lingering in his mind, Ty glanced down the length of the overcrowded car and saw the man in the rear. He wore a black suit, black hat. A scar ran the length of his face. There was a revolver in his hand, but he had not been firing it. Now as mutual recognition struck, he did lift his gun, and Volker fired the length of the aisle at Ty. The bullet tore a rose of splinters from the Pullman's wall beside Ty's head.

Ty could not fire back, not with the men and women crowded along the length of the car. He started that way, angrily shoving a man aside, but before he had taken three strides, Volker had flung open the rear door of the Pullman and vanished into the tumult beyond.

Ty continued in that direction but Sperry grabbed his arm.

"What are you doing!"

"It was Volker. I saw him," Ty said, twisting free of the ranger's grip.

"What good would it do you to chase him?" Sperry said angrily. "Outside they'll shoot you down before you can take two strides."

Rational thinking returned as the flush of anger faded. He nodded gratefully to Sperry. "Have you people come up with a plan back here?"

"Only to try to survive. The outlaws may give up on the idea of robbing the passengers now that every armed man aboard has been alerted. They can see the soldiers from Camp Grant out there as well. They'll likely hit the freight car, blow the safe, then ride like hell with whatever they can grab."

Ty thought that Sperry was probably right. "If the army had attacked we might have driven them off by now," he said, crouching slightly to peer out the window despite the threat of flying bullets from outside.

"If Colonel Toomey is leading them personally, they might never advance," Sperry said. "The old man wouldn't want to end his career by getting himself shot up."

Ty had been shoveling fresh cartridges into his Winchester's tube magazine. Now he took up a shooting position again, saying to Sperry, "All we can do is hold them back and pray for the Rangers."

"I wish there were more of us . . . Cope Michaels is dead. First volley got him. Damned old desert rat."

Ty made no response. Sperry expected none, but the regret he felt over his long-time partner's death was obvious.

"Here they come again," Ty said. He was now on the side of the train where Dink's company—his own men— were bunched. Dink's tactics, as opposed to Skaggs', sent his outlaws at them in skirmish lines. They made brief, deadly forays and then retreated to regroup. Now a line of Shadow Riders rode past Ty's position, firing at the windows of the Pullman. The method was reminiscent of a band of Cheyenne warriors attacking a circled wagon train. Ty shot the first man he aimed at, seeing him fall beneath his horse.

It was the stuttering outlaw, Chipper, that had gone down, and behind him rode his hero, the would-be traitor, Beech. Ty levered a fresh round into the breach of the rifle, fired and cursed silently as this shot went wild, hitting nothing.

Four more Shadow Riders flashed past the window and Ty managed to get off two quick shots which seemed to do little damage. Then a jolting roar slammed him to the floor of the Pullman. Deafening thunder rippled across the shuddering railroad car. The entire Pullman seemed to lift a few inches from the tracks beneath and then slam back down on the rails. Sperry was still beside Ty, bracing himself on the back of a cushionless seat.

"It seems they just blew the freight car," Sperry said laconically.

"Were any of our people inside it?"

"Four men—it'll be a miracle if any of them survived that blast. That was a hell of a lot of dynamite, Ty."

Now the outlaws on both sides withdrew a little, though their gunfire still peppered the train, ricochets whining angrily through the Pullman's interior.

Sperry commented unnecessarily. "He's going to take the gold and make a run for it. We're probably safe now."

"Sure we are," Ty said, anxiously watch the roaring flames beyond the rear of the Pullman blaze away as the front car was devoured by fire. They were trapped if the flames jumped to this car—and there seemed little doubt that they would. Ty found himself wishing that Volker's men would just grab their gold and flee as quickly as possible. He no longer cared about the battle's outcome, but about preserving the lives of those who remained trapped inside the passenger car.

A distant, unnatural sound met Ty's ears. Something that should have been quite normal in its place and time, but bizarre under these circumstances. He looked up again at Sperry's smoke-streaked face and asked, "Does Ethan happen to have a bugler with him?"

"Ethan? No, he never has before. But, come to think of it

Sam McGraw had a man . . ." The sound of the bugle, much nearer now, rang clearly across the smoky battlefield. "They're coming, Ty! The Rangers are here. Now those dogs will find out what real fighting is."

In a matter of minutes the shape of the battle shifted dramatically. Ethan Payne's Rangers struck with their full force, Colonel Toomey's soldiers, seemingly emboldened by the success of the rangers, mounted a charge from their position in the hills. Bullets still flew madly from all sides, but few if any were now aimed at the Pullman car. Risking a look out, Ty saw the outlaws begin to scatter, winging wild shots at the onrushing Rangers as they fled.

"Let's go," Ty said to Sperry as he started toward the back door of the passenger car.

"Wait a minute," Sperry said. "Take this. You'll be glad you did." He handed Ty a long white silk scarf similar to the one he wore. "It was Cope's," Sperry said as Ty knotted the scarf around his throat.

"Mr. Steele," Ty said to the railroad boss in passing, "It's over, I think. But don't let anyone go out until we're sure it's safe. Unless the fire leaves you no choice."

Ty stepped onto the platform and swung to the sandy ground. He shouldered his rifle and levered six rapid shots in the direction of the retreating outlaws. He hit nothing, but sending lead after them relieved some of his anger and frustration. In a crouch he and Sperry moved toward the first freight car. Smoke from the explosion still lingered in the air. The wooden door of the car lay in splinters scattered across the desert sand. Sperry hopped up into the ruined car and returned in moments, shaking his head.

"The blast got the boys, all four of 'em," he reported morosely.

"They took the gold?" Ty asked.

"'Course." Sperry looked shaky now. Ty slapped him on the shoulder. "Come on. Let's see if we can find Ethan and a couple of horses."

"Go on, Ty," Sperry said with an uncharacteristic lack of enthusiasm. "I've had enough."

Ty left Sperry to mourn his dead friends and began walking to the rear of the train. He halted beside the caboose to watch the army of Rangers whipping their ponies past, pursuing the fleeing outlaws. Ethan Payne was not among them. On the far side of the railroad car, Ty found the ranger captain sitting on the bottom rail of the caboose's ladder. His face was pale, dust-streaked. A man Ty did not know was tying a bandage around Captain Payne's left leg. Payne looked up and offered Ty a weak smile.

"Glad to see you made it, Ty."

"Is it bad?" Ty asked, nodding at the leg wound. Ethan smiled grimly.

"Can't tell through all the blood."

"He'll make it," the medic assured Ty.

"I need a horse, Captain," Ty said.

"You can use mine," Payne said. "I won't be riding for a while, but what . . . ?"

"I'm going after him," Ty said. "I want Volker's scalp."

"Leave it to the Rangers, Ty! You're not in any shape to do it."

"I have to do it myself," Ty said grimly.

"They'll get him, Ty!" Payne repeated, wincing as the

medic tightened the knot on his bandage. "The army has sealed off the trails to the outlaw stronghold by now. The Rangers will get Volker. He has no place to go."

"Yes," Ty said, "he does have a place, and I know where it is."

"Wait then. My men will return."

"In a few hours?" Ty asked. "They might be chasing the Shadow Riders all afternoon, for days perhaps. Volker won't be among them. He's too smart for that. No, I know where he's riding and I'm going after him."

Ethan tested his leg and then stood shakily, facing Ty. He asked quietly, "Does it involve the woman? Will he be going to where 'Bert' is?"

"I think so."

Ethan's expression hardened, "Then get riding. God's sake, don't let anything stop you!" The urgency in the captain's voice startled Ty. For a moment he paused, wanting to ask more, but Payne was now insistent.

"Get him, Ty. He'll kill that woman as sure as you're born!"

Ty found Payne's tall Appaloosa pony tethered near and he swung up, heeling the horse sharply. Riding past Payne, he saw the old man's set face, the hardness in his eyes and he wondered what it was that Payne had not had the time to tell him. Why was he sure that Volker was after Dahlia? Or was it Bobbi that Volker meant to revenge himself on? Had he discovered somehow that the women had been the conduit for passing information about the Shadow Riders to law enforcement?

He *knew* somehow that Volker, having seen his plan fall

apart, would have headed for Dahlia's house, leaving the Rangers to be kept busy with the fleeing outlaws. Volker would have a few chosen men with him, and the bulk of the gold from the freight car. The outlaw chief had planned his last big holdup well, and as thorough as he was, Volker would have allowed for any contingency including the ambush he had run into. He would not have cared what happened to his dispersed force of men, only that his own saddlebags were filled with gold.

Loyalty had always been of immense importance to Volker, a word he repeated endlessly, to his lieutenants, his men. If Volker had somehow discovered that Dahlia and Bobbi had been the cause of his downfall, Payne seemed to believe Volker would take the time to revenge himself upon the women. Captain Payne seemed to have meant more than that, however.

No matter, Volker must be found and quickly—ridden down and dispatched like the mad dog he was. Ty rode on, whipping the Appaloosa with his reins. He did not take the time to look for tracks as he crossed the desert. Volker would not have ridden directly to Dahlia's, but would have taken some circuitous route. He had a head start on Ty, but Volker's greed would slow him down. His horse and that of any men he might have picked to ride with him would be weighted down by gold and forced to travel with less speed than the outlaw chief would have wished. There were other horses at Dahlia's ranch. Switching saddles to these fresh ponies would put Volker in a position to easily outdistance any pursuing men from the army or the Arizona Rangers on their own exhausted mounts.

Ty no longer flagged the laboring Appaloosa with his reins as he rode, but he silently urged the tough, rangy animal to run on with whatever strength it had left.

Bobbi. Ty could not keep her out of his thoughts. Was she even at Dahlia's house? He believed it probable. She would have known that almost the entire outlaw camp had moved out and seen her chance. If she had delayed for whatever reason, by now the army would have crushed the outlaw resistance at the foot of the back trail, and she could have slipped out that way. Ty felt sure that she had ridden to join her sister, perhaps to urge Dahlia to flee with her.

Dahlia had four or five men on her ranch, including the big man, Eric. But were they loyal to Dahlia or to Volker? It would be child's play for Volker to make his way to the ranch house and remove any opposition by men who would not expect him to turn his guns on them.

Ty ascended the last rise on the staggering Appaloosa. The horse needed to rest, but could not be allowed to rest. Not a mile away now he could see Dahlia's white house sitting on its surrounding bench, the sun gleaming brightly across its face. Ty could see no sign of activity; not a man or a horse revealed itself. Apologizing to the big appaloosa for its ill-treatment, he rode on, his face a smoke-smeared mask of bitter determination.

Half a mile on, Ty cut sign. Three horses, all carrying heavy loads, judging by the depth of their hoofprints in the sandy soil. Ty circled across them, working his way toward the rear of the house. His heart gave a little leap when he spotted the big black stallion standing shuddering, frothing in the yard.

Ty dismounted, slapping the Appy on the rump to send it away. With the sun-heated Winchester in his hand, Ty wove his way through the creosote and sagebrush surrounding the house. He was half a dozen running strides from the open back door when four gunshots rang out. A shadow appeared in the doorway and Ty lifted his rifle to his shoulder, but did not fire, unsure of his target.

The shadowy figure backed from the house, holding his stomach with both hands. The big man, Eric turned unseeing eyes on Ty and then fell over, dead. Ty recklessly rushed the door, fear knotting his dry throat.

Inside the shadowed house, he turned aside and ducked low, but there were no more shots. He could hear voices somewhere, a heavy commanding voice followed by a tearful wail. Ty was in a large kitchen with a heavy-beamed ceiling. An interior door stood open. He took a moment to orient himself, trying to remember the layout of the house. Down the corridor revealed by the open door, Bobbi's bedroom lay to the left, Dahlia's to the right. Beyond these was the front room, the parlor where Champ had been doctored, to its right . . . He thought.

The deep voice shouted out again. There was a loud slap, flesh meeting flesh, and then again a fearful cry. Ty plunged ahead into the depths of the house.

The bedroom doors right and left stood open on empty rooms. The front door to the big house was open to the desert day, the sun casting brilliant white shapes about the room beyond.

Dahlia was seated on the parlor floor, her knees drawn up, hands to her face. The sleeve of her dark green dress had been torn away revealing her white shoulder, and her blond hair lay in a tangle around her face. Volker hovered over her, his shoulders hunched with anger. When he spun to face Ty, his snake eyes were glitter-bright, totally mad. Ty saw the outlaw's hand come up and he dove behind the red settee as Volker's Colt boomed. The bullet flew past Ty, breaking a window, and Volker began to laugh wildly, insanely.

"Here it is, Ranger, come and get it!" Volker shouted. Ty was positioning himself, ready to make his move, when he saw, from the corner of his eye, a second shadowy figure behind him. Trapped, Ty spun that way. As he moved two pistol shots rang out so closely together that they sounded as one and Ty saw the man who had entered the front door collapse onto the polished oak floor.

Champ! Ty took in the sprawled outlaw at a glance. He lay unmoving, his silver-banded hat beneath him. Cursing silently Ty popped up from behind the settee, his rifle at the ready. He was too late.

Volker was already down. Studdard's shot had sent a bullet ripping through the scarred outlaw's face and skull, killing him instantly. Dahlia screamed and tried to struggle to her feet. Dropping his rifle, Ty went to the blond woman and helped her to rise.

"It's all right, Dahlia . . ." he said, trying to comfort her, but she struggled free of his arms and rushed to where Champ lay, collapsing on her knees beside him, petting his head.

The voice beyond them was low and menacing, too familiar.

"That just leaves the two of us, doesn't it?" Wynn

Corby said as he stepped into the room from the porch beyond and stood silhouetted by the white desert light behind him.

Corby still wore the army uniform he had worn in the
raid on the train. The redhead was hatless, trail-dusty and
he wore a twisted, menacing grin. Corby, in uniform once
again, resembled the frightened young soldier Ty had taken
under his wing, but Wynn was hard and older now.

Ty tried talking to him. "It's over, Wynn. Take your
chance to ride now before they hang you or stand you up
in front of a firing squad."

"What're you afraid of, Ty?" Wynn laughed humor-
lessly. "Afraid I'm going to kill you? You wouldn't buck me
before, remember." He nodded at the unmoving body of
Studdard. "He had to pull you out of the fight. Hell, I see it
now, Ty. You're afraid of me. You always have been ever
since I showed you that I had it in me to bash Spud's head
in with a rock. You stopped me that night, but I got Spud in
the end. I always finish what I start . . . in the end."

With that, Corby started his draw, but he flinched just a
little, and it was too late by the time he drew the hammer
of his Colt back and brought the muzzle level. Ty's gun
had already erupted with savage effectiveness and Wynn,
blinking his eyes as if he could clear the death from them,
fell over, his pistol clattering to the floor beside him. A
deep silence settled across the room. Dahlia was sobbing
silently.

"Anyone else around, Dahlia?" Ty asked without holstering his gun, and the blond woman, Champ's head cra-

dled in her arms, replied in a grief-strangled voice, "No one. All dead. No one here."

"I'm still here," Bobbi said.

Ty felt the blood rush to his head. Bobbi in jeans and a red shirt, stood in the bright sunshine just beyond the doorway. Her hair was wind-tangled, her smile uncertain as she looked around at the carnage.

"It looks like I got here too late," Bobbi said, coming into the room. She rested her hand on Dahlia's shoulder, but her wide brown eyes were only on Ty.

"Not too late," he muttered. Stepping forward, he held out his arms and she ran to him to be tightly embraced. Relief, concern, deep needful caring all rushed through Ty. Their embrace was long, a comfort, a promise. "Just in time, Bobbi," he whispered. "You came just in time."

Chapter Thirteen

Dusk had brought color to the western sky and a cooling breeze drifted through the open door of Dan McGraw's office. Scattered about the room, those gathered listened to Ethan Payne as he finished summarizing the day's events for those who had not been present.

"Only a handful of the Shadow Riders escaped," Payne was saying as he sat, wounded leg propped up, a coffee cup between his hands. "They're scattered along the border now. It's unlikely they'll show their faces up here again, any of them."

"Much of the gold missing?" Ben Sperry asked. He stood in the corner of the room. His mustache was waxed to perfection, but he no longer wore his white silk scarf.

"Very little, Ben," Payne replied. "Volker managed to keep the bulk of it with him. Probably he told his men that they would meet later to split it up. Which, of course, he would not have done. This was to be his last raid—he had plans to retire in Virginia. The purchase agreement for a house and land were found in his office safe here in town."

"Will the railroad continue to operate—after this?" Bobbi asked. All eyes went to the brown-eyed woman who sat demurely beside Ty. She wore a blue dress with a hint of lace at the throat. Ty sat perched on the corner of McGraw's desk, his eyes watching her with fond possessiveness.

"It looks like it," McGraw answered. "I talked to Allison Steele of the A&E. He is a determined cuss. They're only waiting to have a new locomotive shuttled down here. They are going to review their security, however."

McGraw glanced at Ty and said, "Steele mentioned something about there being a good job for you with the railroad if you were so inclined."

"No, thanks!" Ty said emphatically. "I doubt I'll ever ride the rails again. Besides," he said inclining his head, "Bobbi and I have other plans."

"So we gathered," Captain Payne muttered with a crooked smile. "What is it you two are planning to do, Ty?"

Bobbi leaned forward, hands between her knees and said, "The ranch, of course! I haven't waited this long and had Ty fight so hard just to give it up. We're going ranching, aren't we?" she asked, looking up at Ty who nodded his assent.

"We'll be staying in town until we can build a house," Ty added.

"There's a fine house on the property already, isn't there?" Sperry asked.

"Volker's house!" Bobbi said, her eyes flashing. "I wouldn't spend a night in it! We're going to set fire to it or tear it down for the lumber."

"That and the barracks," Ty agreed. "We'll build a new bunkhouse for any ranch hands we might take on later. Uncle Morgan and Judd will keep on living in the old stone house if they choose to stay."

Ty and Bobbi had agreed that they wanted nothing remaining that reminded them of Volker and the Shadow Riders. It was an expensive decision to make, but Ethan thought he understood it. Living in a house haunted by Mingo and his terrible past was not something he, himself, would care for.

"What about your sister?" Ethan asked, "Will she be staying with you or remain where she was living?"

"Neither for the time being. She needs some time alone just now. I doubt she'll choose to go back to her old house, though," Bobbi said.

Ethan nodded his understanding. Champ Studdard had died in her arms there. He considered, however, that maybe that had been the best, the only resolution their doomed love affair could have found. Champ would certainly have been arrested and sent to prison for many years even if he had not been sentenced to hang. No matter how the world had judged him, though, Dahlia had loved him and she was shattered. She was now staying in a hotel room in town while she decided what it was she wanted for her future.

"Ty," Ethan said with gravity, "there's someone I'd like you to talk to. You and me alone."

"Oh?" Ty frowned slightly, glanced at Bobbi and said, "All right, if you say so, Ethan."

"It won't take long," Payne told Bobbi. "It's just something that still needs to be cleared up."

Bobbi glanced at Ty who shrugged. She agreed with some disappointment. "If it's not for long," she said. "We were going . . ."

"I'll be back in time to take you to dinner," Ty promised.

Ethan had struggled to his feet with Sperry's help and now stood waiting with the aid of his new crutch, his own face quite serious. Ty decided that whatever it was that Payne had in mind, it wasn't going to be much fun for him. He whispered a promise to Bobbi, grabbed his hat and followed the hobbling Payne out the door into the twilight.

"Come on," Payne said, and he led the way down the plank walk, swinging unevenly on his crutch. The building they entered was just three doors down from McGraw's office. Inside Ty saw the back of a seated man. A single low lantern burned, casting dim yellow across the room.

Ethan stopped at the threshold and gripped Ty's arm tightly. "Ty—you have to promise me you won't lose your temper."

Ty's frown deepened, but he nodded his agreement to the ranger captain and they entered the room as the uniformed man rose from the leather chair to greet them.

"Deveraux!" Ty said explosively as the army lieutenant from Camp Grant came forward. The man with the cleft chin, the narrow mouth concealed by the shaggy black mustache, and unyielding eyes did not smile. He nodded, however, to Payne.

"Thank you, sir," Colonel Toomey's aide said in a low voice devoid of inflection. "Will you gentlemen have a seat?"

Ty felt his muscles bunch as he continued to look into the eyes of the man who had abused Corby, had sentenced them to the hot box, to the unending torment of the road gang. Ethan touched Ty's arm again, reminding him of his promise.

"I'll stand," Ty said. Deveraux shrugged as if it made no difference to him one way or the other. The two men stood, eyes locked, and Ethan decided to break the mood if he could.

"Ty, let's set a few things straight before you say whatever it is you might wish to Deveraux. First of all, Lieutenant Deveraux had absolutely no connection with the Shadow Riders. It was Colonel Toomey who began working with Volker to use men from the stockade as recruits for the outlaws.

"The colonel was near retirement, in ill-health. His hopes of making brigadier general before he did retire had been crushed. It was a way for him to make money and rid his command of troublemakers at the same time."

"You were commanding the army force when the train was attacked today, weren't you?" Ty demanded of Deveraux. "If your men had charged earlier, lives could have been saved."

"My orders—from Toomey—were to hold back and supply cover," Deveraux said without a glimmer of shame.

To
Tempt
a
Rogue

Connie Mason

Thorndike Press • Waterville, Maine

This is a work of fiction. Names, characters, places, and incidents are products of the author's imagination or are used fictitiously and are not to be construed as real. Any resemblance to actual events, locales, organizations, or persons, living or dead, is entirely coincidental.

Published in 2002 by arrangement with Avon Books, an imprint of HarperCollins Publishers, Inc.

Thorndike Press Large Print Basic Series.

The tree indicium is a trademark of Thorndike Press.

The text of this Large Print edition is unabridged. Other aspects of the book may vary from the original edition.

Set in 16 pt. Plantin by Myrna S. Raven.

Printed in the United States on permanent paper.

Library of Congress Cataloging-in-Publication Data

Mason, Connie.
    To tempt a rogue / Connie Mason.
      p. cm.
    ISBN 0-7862-3951-4 (lg. print : hc : alk. paper)
    1. Arizona — Fiction. 2. Large type books. I. Title.
PS3563.A78786 T63 2002
  813'.54—dc21   2001054064